THE LAST VILLAGE

Audla English

For my mam,
who always wanted to be in a book.

Before we were conceived, we existed in part as an egg in our mother. All the eggs a woman will ever carry form in her while she is a four-month-old foetus in her mother. This means our cellular life begins in our grandmother. Each of us spent five months in our grandmother and she, in turn, formed within her grandmother. We vibrate to the rhythms of our mother's blood before she herself is born. And this pulse is the thread of blood that runs all the way back through the grandmothers to the first mother.

—LAYNE REDMOND

PROLOGUE

2017

My gran was always an inspirational woman to me but until recently I just never knew how much.

I have always been incredibly close to my gran but I never knew much about her past, a selfishness perhaps of my youth and a foolish belief that the things in my life are the most important. To this day, in my opinion, my gran is just one of those truly exquisite individuals: a humble, loving and kind disposition paired with a fierce independence alongside an ageless beauty. Even now at ninety, her hair colour may have faded, and she may have shrunk in height but her eyes remain just as bright and mahogany as ever before and her cheekbones just as strong.

I, Anna Charles, grew up in the North East of England, I came from a happy home, had a lovely childhood and I have always done everything that was expected of me. I got my GCSE's, followed by my A Levels and then I went to university, applied myself and worked really hard to eventually become a lawyer. I was fortunate enough to be able to get a good job at a local law firm and you could say I lead a very uninteresting regimented life.

It wasn't until I met James that my life felt complete on all levels. A fellow lawyer, we met at a rather tedious law networking event and as the dulcet music played we were two people reaching for the final canapé as our hands touched, a Caribbean spiced fish kebab. We ended up sharing it and perhaps you could say it was our joint love of food which brought us together. We have been a couple for four years now and live in a charming 1930s semi-detached house in the quaint little town of Roker, not far from the city of Sunderland and only five minutes from the beautiful North-East coast.

I have vivid and such cherished memories of spending many of my childhood days at my gran's house in the nearby Whitburn Village. Even now, I still love going to the enchanting little honeysuckle-covered cottage, its path lined with an array of pastel-coloured roses which dance and sway in the wind welcoming you kindly as you make your way along their route. The cottage inside is always overflowing with smiles, a constant smell of fresh coffee, never-ending supply of mouth-watering cooked bacon and fragrant scents of Lily of the Valley, my gran's perfume.

As a child, the numerous enticing curiosities which lined the hallway shelves and peeked out at me, intrigued my thoughts. I used to spend hours imagining what it must be like in those far off exotic places. I spent my childhood time there eating tuna mayonnaise sandwiches, making tents out of old bed sheets, selling homemade pressed rose perfume to the friendly neighbours and playing in the large garden that was joined to the rear of the house.

If I was there on an evening, I was treated to an occasion that my gran called 'a high tea'. This rather delightful affair would involve a proper home-cooked meal which was always served at a properly set table with bread and butter, no matter what it was, a pot of tea with cup and saucer, and a fresh napkin in a napkin ring. My gran truly revelled in my visits. Sometimes she'd let me accompany her for a trip out on the old bus, the number thirty, that went into the town where she would take me to the grand department store Binns, the hustling and bustling heart of the town with its flashy sign and smart façade, where she would buy me juice and a cream cake in its silver service restaurant; it was such a pleasure.

Occasionally, my parents worked away which would secretly delight me as it would mean I would need to have a sleepover. I had my own little bedroom in the cottage, a lovely little sunlit room with views over the sea as far as the eyes could see. The room was only small with one window, enough to fit a single bed, a wardrobe and a set of drawers but I liked to think of it as my cosy palace. On the windowsill sat the majestic chestnut Shire horse ornament, which my gran called Peglets and who used to keep me company.

The walls were decorated colourfully in pink patterned flowers, the bed covered in a swirling whirling pink with a purple handmade woollen throw which felt soft on your skin when you lay on it. I had my own little drawer in that room where I could keep treasures which consisted of my pencils, books and the odd small toy which I had managed to bring as a comforter (especially for sleepovers). As part of my bedtime routine, once I had reached six years old, I was allowed to listen to music on the wireless in my bed. On hot days, when the window was open, this was accompanied by the faint sound of the waves lapping the sea. My gran would then come up to signal lights out and she would hum 'My Bonnie Lies over the Ocean', to me gently stroking my hair until I drifted off to sleep.

In the morning I was forever awoken by those sizzling bacon scents which would nonchalantly drift up the stairs beckoning me to come down and then we would happily chat over breakfast. I solemnly miss those precious days and will never ever forget them; as an adult I can no longer stay at my gran's house anymore, it's just not what you do as a grown up, although sometimes I really wish I could.

As years passed by, I matured, as did the very special, endless, unbreakable love and bond with my gran. She has always been there for me through both happy and sad times. Her caring and loving nature has supported me when we have lost family members, when she herself will have been in deep pain, or when I have had difficult break ups from a past boyfriend or even when I cried from the sad passing of a pet. Thankfully the happier times tremendously outweigh the sad ones; and one of these times was when my closest friend Nora got engaged.

Nora, who lived in the same street as me when I was little, would often also come to my gran's house straight after school and also during holidays as both her parents worked too and we still remain friends to this day. Nora was welcomed with as much gusto as I ever was, with gran setting out endless cups of juice cordial, freshly made sandwiches and home-baked cherry scones. I always remember the day that Nora got engaged, I was absolutely elated for her and I was bursting to tell my gran all about the engagement. However, I remember this day not just for the engagement of my close friend but as the day that my gran started to tell me about her past; her experience of love, a pure and powerful love. It was this same day that I learnt that normal people, people you have known your entire life, often have the most extraordinary story to tell.

It was a cold uneventful rainy September day in 2017; I took my gran to the nearby town, a town she sadly no longer recognised. Binns, the once grand dame of the street, the old department store which held such happy memories for us both, had long since shut down and been cruelly demolished to be replaced with row upon row of generic mundane bargain shops. My gran looked small and downcast as we drove back alongside the seafront so I parked up in the windy grey car park next to the regal Souter Lighthouse, which was a beacon of radiance on that miserable day, to look out at the infinite panorama of the coast.

To try and cheer my gran up, I took and held her lined hand gently and said,

"Gran, I forgot to say, I had some lovely news last night. Nora got engaged, isn't that wonderful?"

My gran clapped her wrinkled hands together happily and a small smile began to form on her face, she seemed genuinely very pleased and we talked for a little while about the excitement and plans that lay ahead for Nora.

As we pondered further, we looked out at the harsh almost grey-looking North Sea and then to the open grassy space that lay behind us, my gran began to relax and to truly allow herself to smile. Her smile was an intriguing smile, a smile which revealed unrivalled memories of her childhood, a smile which illuminated a young woman laughing with her friends, a smile which revealed a young woman in love but also a smile which exposed a longing for the past, her past.

It was then that my gran started to focus her attention to the windswept open field that headed up the cliff with a twinkle in her eyes.

It was then that she began to tell me about her past and life in the village, a lost village, the village of Marsden which used to stand on the very space that we were looking at.

LILY

1933

I had a very cheerful childhood growing up in Marsden. Born in the house I came to live in for the next nineteen years, my dad was a miner whilst my mam kept house, and although we didn't have much, what we did have was each other. My dad was my hero, a big strong fellow who would come back from his day covered in a dark canvass like a shadow from an oil painting, with his hazel eyes piercing through and his hat jaunted to one side over his raven black hair. My mam was the most beautiful woman I have ever laid eyes on, an actual angel, who walked on this earth with her almond-shaped azure eyes, perpetual rosy pink cheeks, red rose bud lips and her crowning glory of honey-coloured hair. My dad was absolutely beguiled by her beauty, a beauty which I would later come to inherit, albeit with different colouring.

Marsden was only a little Northern miner's village but I loved it there. Positioned precariously at the top of a cliff face, the village stared out into a vast landscape of blue wilderness as far as the eye could see. The result of this was that although we experienced harsh ice-cold winters that strode in from the North Sea with breath that would chill the very bones off you, we were also a stone's throw away from a sandy beach, perfect for the hazy summer months. There was a central village green which was surrounded by nine rows of terraced houses all packed in together tightly. The village itself had everything we could ever need: its own church, village shop for supplies, brass band, there was even a small train, but what made our village even more special, was that it was shielded by a glorious lighthouse, Souter Lighthouse. The village harboured its own little devoted community, all families of miners and only those who lived in it could ever understand what it was like.

We lived in one of the miner's terraces, a two-up two-down modest house which was connected to the other terraces or, as I knew and loved them, my extended family. The heart and soul of each of the houses in those days was the downstairs parlour kitchen room with its huge sooty coal fired range. In this multi-faceted stone chamber dishes were concocted, laundry pressed, women would natter, men would rest and children would play. Each house had a small yard which was then connected to a back lane to allow for deliveries into the houses. It was always such an exciting commotion when the different carts would enter the village; twice per week the fishmonger would come with his abundance of freshly caught delights from the North Sea and once per week the butcher from nearby Whitburn would come with his range of meats. I also looked forward to Fridays when the smartly dressed tea man would come to the village with his lovely little van and knock on our door with his wicker basket adorned with fresh teas, biscuits and jams. My mam used to always buy the tea like this. It was always a treat when there were biscuits in the house; it was simple lovely pleasures those days. As the terraces didn't have gardens, all the miners were allocated a small patch of land in the allotment that lay to the base of the lighthouse. I spent many a day there with my dad helping him grow all sorts of vegetables, such as potatoes, turnips and carrots and he even let me have one of his old shovels. It is surprising really to think back at how well they grew given the land had the sea directly underneath it with its bitter salt air. I always liked to imagine that the glow of the lighthouse helped them grow.

I have very vivid memories of my childhood, most of them involving my childhood friends Nell and Harry. We were a mighty trio us three and we thought we could take on the world and we so frequently did. Our trio formed on the first day of infant school, the lovely little grey brick building that lay in the shadow of the lighthouse. It was only a short walk from my house and I would always meet Harry on the way. His dad was the train driver, or as we knew it the Rattler driver, and he lived in the house at the end of our terrace. Harry was my closest friend; he was short, like me and had dark brown almost raven-coloured hair like me too, we used to look like quite a pair and would like to pretend we were brother and sister. On our first day, we excitedly and busily got into a line at the school ready to go in not knowing what to expect with this new adventure. It was then that the girl in front of us turned around; it was Nell.

Nell was the daughter of the lighthouse keeper at Souter, a heart-shaped face framed by white blonde hair and with a wild untamed spirit in her eyes. To this day I still think Harry fell in love with her from the first moment he saw her. There were only thirty children in the school and we used to do our daily lessons and go to the little church across the road for morning prayers. The school days dragged on and we yearned for the holidays in much the same way as all young children do.

The summer holidays were the best holidays of them all. When the North Sea was kind, we spent the days on the half sandy, half shingle beach at Marsden. The beach was hidden within a headland, if you didn't live locally you didn't know about it. To reach it we would climb down almost two hundred precarious looking white painted stairs, an escapade in itself for young children. The beach also concealed some further hidden treasures, an intertwining maze of sea caves who glared out at a vast blue wilderness with a rock monument jutting out and breaking their vision. This natural phenomenon was known as Marsden Rock and its unsupported arch made it look like a lower-case 'n'. Nell always said it was put there for her as it was the main thing you could see looking out of her lighthouse window. The rock was home to hundreds upon hundreds of sea birds. You could always hear their shrill calls the moment you entered the steps. The other thing the beach had was a pub, The Beach Grotto, can you believe it? A pub at the bottom of all those steps! My dad always relayed forgotten tales with us children listening to his every word with wide eyes, saying that The Beach Grotto used to be a pirates' meeting place and they used to hide all their stolen goods in the caves which they would blast out with dynamite. I never knew whether to believe him though. I always wondered how they got the beer barrels down there and it wasn't until much later that I discovered there was a lift.

We used to spend hours on that beach – me, Nell, and Harry. We would play hide and seek in the caves, we would make firm sand pies (even better using the clay sand at the bottom of the cliffs), swim in the sea and look for winkles in the pebbles. On very glorious days old Mr Tony would come down to the beach from nearby South Shields with his wheelbarrow of ice creams, chirpily singing away in his delightful language whilst twirling his jet-black feathery moustache, the ice cream was even more delicious back then and flavours like cinder toffee and granny's apple would melt in your mouth as tiny zests burst out as you ate more. There were no health and safety rules in those days and children were free to just enjoy the simple indulgence of ice cream on a sunny day.

Sometimes when we were brave we would even try to swim out to the Rock to get a closer look at the seabirds. Nell was forever climbing up into nooks and crevices, frequently one-handed, to help baby gulls who had fallen from their nests. Harry used to watch her with a look of sheer terror, madness and total admiration when she did this but she never fell. We always felt safe on the beach with the red and white stripes of Souter Lighthouse peering down and watching over us.

On our way back up the white stairs and heading home, we would often see old Peglets, the majestic Shire horse, eating grass at the top of the cliff. Peglets was Mr Brigg's horse and he worked with my dad at the mine and delivered the coal around the nearby villages. Nell always loved animals so we used to give Peglets a good pat whilst Mr Briggs was having a drink in The Beach Grotto on his way home after a long day's work. Sometimes if we were lucky, Harry's dad, Mr Gunn would see us and would let us jump on the back of the old Rattler to get a lift back to the village. The Rattler, as it was lovingly known, was a small steam train which would take the freshly mined coal, the black gold, all the way from the mine to the town. A rackety old bone shaking journey which engulfed your whole body with its slightly warm, smoky, and sweet air but one I would not change in a million years.

On rainy days, we would go to the lighthouse. Nell's parents, Mr and Mrs Green, would welcome us in and it was like stepping into a giant red and white stripy pawn chess piece. The three of us children would spiral up to the very top, over one hundred tiny stairs and Mr Green would let us sit up there with him. An electric lighthouse, the first of its kind in the world, how lucky were we. I remember days when the three of us would even do our homework up there in that cosy little space looking out at the immense sea, our faces illuminated by the dull shine of the lighthouse beam.

We would also often help Mr Green clean the windows right up at the top and make them really gleam, a very important task so that the sailors would be able to see where the mainland was. This used to be quite an effort in itself, to get the water and soap up all of those spiralling stairs using the various pulleys and contraptions put in place to allow for this. We would always end up drenched in water and soap suds, but it was so much fun.

The other thing in the lighthouse which always caught our attention were the funny looking tubes which hung on the wall in the lantern room. We came to discover that these were speaking tubes. These were connected to various rooms around the lighthouse and on clear days we would send Harry to the engine room whilst Nell and I stayed in the lantern. We would take it in turns to play, 'Guess the animal' using the tubes to ask each other questions to guess which animal we were pretending to be. We used to think this was marvellous! Sometimes we would put our drinks and snacks orders in with Harry and he would always bring our wishes up to the lantern room. We had to be careful playing with the speaking tubes as really, we should not have touched them. One day we got into serious trouble when we played and picked up the wrong speaking tube which connected to Nell's mam and dad's bedroom. Mrs Green was really not amused by Harry and myself making elephant noises at her down the tube when she was cleaning the room. We felt embarrassed and somewhat bashful for weeks after that one.

The winter days were a stark contrast. A frozen icy imp would leap out of the sea, glistening the entire village. Heavy curtains were drawn. My mam was always cheerful as she loved the winter months despite the cold, she used to call it her hibernation time and she would play music on the wireless whilst doing her ironing, swaying and humming from side to side in time to the rhythm with each press she made. My dad would always come in after work and wrap his freezing cold arms around her and give her an affectionate hug and a kiss. I remember she used to laugh, the sweetest sound ever and call him her giant sooty ice block and tell him to get in the bath before he put muck on her freshly pressed clothes. She would always have a hot bath and a meal ready for him when he came home from the mine. My favourite dish she did was Pan Haggerty, a true winter's dish using all the leftover meat and any vegetables you could get your hands on from the allotment. This would warm you through from the tip of your toes to the last length of hair on your head.

I still pine for those days of joy, an uncomplicated life of fun with Nell and Harry and the warm love and devotion of my parents.

ANNA

January 2017

I have been looking forward to this evening for a long time.

James and I were finally going to try the new restaurant in Newcastle that I had read so much about. We had both been working really long hours recently, so James suggested that we stay over in Newcastle and really enjoy our meal with a nice bottle of wine without worrying about finding an extortionately priced taxi and fretting about getting home. The restaurant was on the top floor of a prestigious gallery which promised to offer panoramic views of the river, bridges and the Newcastle skyline. I could not imagine a more perfect place to eat, an amalgamation of my great loves in life: James, food, art and the North East of England.

We decided to get to the hotel early to check in, so that we could treat it like a tiny holiday, we could get dressed there and then make our way leisurely over to the restaurant. The hotel directly faced the art gallery and restaurant from across the river and could be reached by foot by the Millennium Bridge, a display of art in herself. Possessing some real curves, she looked like an oval-shaped metallic eye who had the ability to wink at you if a ship needed to pass. In the evening the bridge would light up and it looked as if she was wearing a fluctuating neon-coloured eyeliner, perhaps preparing herself for the lively Newcastle nightlife.

In our soft grey and chicly designed room, we sampled some of the miniature delights out of the shiny small fridge and snacked on some peanuts. I really have terrible willpower and can't help myself around these bite-size treats of snacks and liquor and James is no better. I wore my favourite midnight blue dress paired with a long gold necklace and gold stiletto heels; it was also one of James's favourites as he thought it 'highlighted' my curves as it was knee length and tight, quite different to my usual daily office clothes. I wore my golden hair loose and painted on a simple bright red lip to finish my look.

As we got ready to leave our sumptuous hotel room for the evening which lay ahead, James strode over to me gathered me in his arms and kissed me.

"Anna, you look absolutely perfect," he whispered in my ear as he took my hand and led me out to go to the restaurant. I think James had also been looking forward to tonight as he looked even more amazing than usual in a blue suit making his eyes look even bluer. I looked up and down the energetic riverside with its trendy bars and nightspots as we made the short walk across the Millennium Bridge and into the art gallery. I inhaled all the colours of the modern art pieces which danced about like firecrackers in front of me before we got into the lift to get to the 8th floor and the restaurant.

Once there I could not believe the views; it was like sitting within our own personal painting. A skyline as far as the eye could see as the bridges of Newcastle stood proudly over the river with the cheeky Millennium Bridge giving me a pink neon wink as if she was trying to tell me something and at the same time courteously letting a spirited party boat pass beneath her. The silver shimmering beetle-like concert hall on the same side of the river reflected the last outings of the September sun producing iridescent beams of light over the grand Newcastle quayside with the old chimneys of the timeworn Victorian buildings peeping up through the horizon.

The maitre d' beckoned for us and as we took our seats, James ordered us a bottle of pink champagne, my favourite and an absolute treat. As we clinked our glasses and let the bubbles tickle our tongues with their sharp fresh taste, we talked about everything whilst the hustle and bustle of the busy restaurant passed us by, our house, our families, our jobs. I spoke about my gran and also about Nora and her upcoming wedding and we raised a toast to life. For dinner, we began with the goat's cheese bruschetta drizzled with a balsamic glaze with the creamy cheese oozing over the lightly oiled aromatic bread, murmuring, we both agreed how the smooth cheese just melted in our mouths. I followed this with salmon and pink peppercorns which was divine, especially when sipping the pink champagne; whilst James ordered steak in a red wine sauce, his favourite. We finished with a tangy chocolate orange fondant oozing a smooth milk chocolate layer and softening in our mouths with surprising little bursts of zesty citrus. We then headed back to the hotel bar for a night cap.

As we sauntered merrily to get the lift back down to the hotel, I leaned into James's muscular body and whispered to him.

"James this has been the most perfect evening. It's just what we both need, thank you."

He kissed my forehead lovingly as he wrapped his arms around me and we had a precious moment as we descended from the deep pink sky to the twinkling lights of the city below.

We walked over the glimmering silver lit pavement and up to the inviting Millennium Bridge which was now immersed in a deep blue. James turned and smiled at me.

"Anna, the blue light is beaming off your dress, you look unreal. Let's go to the middle of the bridge so I can take a photo with all the bridges in the background. It'll be a great memory of tonight."

We ambled to the middle of the bridge taking in the fresh evening air, as we got there James said, "Anna, go and stand there next to the bridge in the middle of the walkway and I will get the camera set up ready to take a photo." I turned around to walk to the bridge, giddy on life remembering this wonderful evening and then I turned back to James to pose for a photo and I was shocked beyond my core.

There was James, my confidante, partner in crime and fellow food critic and he was facing me but was down on one knee. I didn't know whether to laugh or cry.

James confidently said, "Anna Charles, love of my life, my beautiful girl, will you marry me?"

I am not ashamed to admit it, but I shrieked, a mixture of utter shock and absolute joy. For a moment I didn't know what to say and I had an almost out-of-body experience as I took in James's wonderful words, until I looked down at poor James's waiting and eager face.

"Yes James, of course I will marry you," I said loudly.

James then slipped the most flawless looking marquise cut sapphire ring onto my finger, the stone for September my birthday month and we embraced. I couldn't believe we were engaged to be married.

As we got back to the hotel I was so excited and James suggested we just go back to the room to celebrate. As I opened the door and switched the light on, there in the middle of the room was a beautiful bouquet of vibrant pink roses and a new bottle of pink champagne which was chilling in a silver ice bucket, as my ring caught the light and reflected a beautiful blue glow onto it. I realised that James, the swine, must have been planning it all along even down to the picture of my shocked face. I couldn't wait to tell all my family about it.

I woke up the following morning a bit parched and with a little bit of a headache, as I stretched my arms up over my head my hand got caught as I tried to move the hair which had fallen over my face. It all came rushing back to me as I looked down at my ring finger, I clenched my teeth with delight as I looked next to my gorgeous sleeping fiancé as he lay next to me. As James woke up, my headache started to fade as I kissed him. I wanted to invite the two families round to our house that afternoon to share our news, which James thought was a lovely idea. I set to ringing around the two families to suggest an afternoon gathering. I knew they would question why we were doing this out of the blue but I didn't let on the reason. I also rang Nora, as my closest friend, and her fiancé Tim to invite them, I knew she would be overjoyed for us and I was eager to tell her. I also had the romantic notion that it would be a special time for us as friends to share ideas and be able to look forward to our upcoming weddings together.

As we drove home, James and I stopped at the local delicatessen to pick up a quiche, any pie slices that they had on short notice and a selection of their delicious home-made cakes. We then went to the nearby supermarket and bought a case of prosecco. I felt so grown up as I unloaded the car into our house and started to lay the delicacies out onto the dining room table in preparation for our announcement.

Just after three p.m., as our loved ones all started to pile in, our two families together, James and I gathered them all in the garden and faced them.

"Surprise!" we shouted together. "We got engaged last night."

The sound echoed throughout our garden as our families whooped with joy. My mam burst into tears and everyone was so incredibly happy for us. The prosecco flowed freely amongst the guests as the two families wanted to hear about the proposal. My parents took James and I to one side as my mam pulled a card for our engagement out of her bag. James had already asked my dad's permission for my hand in marriage and I was very moved by this gesture from him and I knew then that my parents had been in on the proposal.

Nora, who was knocking back the prosecco at quite a rate throughout the afternoon, teetered over to me and James in her high heels as she flung her arms around us both.

"Congratulations to you both," she said, as she stumbled a little in her shoes.

"Anna, let me see the ring again," and she grabbed a hold of my finger. Nora surveyed my finger coolly as she made out a little sigh.

"It is lovely, Anna," Nora remarked, "but it's not a diamond is it?" and she laughed as if to cover up her comment as a joke, before flouncing back off to Tim.

I was really taken aback by Nora's comment about my ring. I looked at James who looked back at me in fury.

"'I am sure she didn't mean it as it came out," I said to James. "I think she has had too much to drink."

James rolled his eyes at me. I took his hand and said, "Nora is just jealous, and I love my ring and the effort you must have gone into to pick it for me: this is much more meaningful and personal to me, rather than how she just picked out her ring herself."

James sighed and went off to talk to his family. I was not going to let Nora spoil our party and I felt sure that she didn't mean it. Also, Nora was my oldest and closest friend and I had already asked her to be a bridesmaid at our wedding.

I went and sat with my gran who was smiling at me from the tall old wicker chair which overlooked the garden. There was just something about my gran which could always make me feel happy and at peace with myself, a very special bond between generations. She took my hand and examined the ring in detail.

"That is beautiful, pet," she said with her aged gentle voice. "What a sparkler! James is a very lucky man to be marrying our lovely Anna."

As the scent of Lily of the Valley drifted over me, she leaned in to kiss me on the cheek. I looked at her elderly wise face and realised she had that look in her eye again and I knew she was thinking of the village.

LILY

September 1945

The last few years have been extremely difficult. I am incredibly thankful that times are now changing and are at a point where we can move on but will never forget. The mine resumed full capacity after the war and normal service continued once again in the village. Souter Lighthouse shone brightly once more and we could enjoy being a trio again.

We had reached adulthood now – Nell and Harry and I – and we had formed an unbreakable bond. Nell had blossomed even more to become an astonishingly stunning young woman with her white blonde hair continuing to frame her face atop her willowy height. This was in stark contrast to me, so we looked quite a duo! I had remained short and exceptionally dark and had become quite womanly. If I was to describe us from a distance, Nell was like a fashion mannequin whereas I was more like a little pin-up. The biggest change of all however, was in Harry.

Harry had developed to become a six-foot two tall muscularly built man, muscles earned as a result of pure hard labour as during the war Harry had helped whenever he could in the mine and with his father on the Rattler.

During the war, the whole close-knit community worked together and Nell and I had also helped in whichever ways we could. I was never far away from the school supporting and aiding the children in their learning and I helped with the Sunday school at the church whenever possible. Despite what was going on in the outside world and the difficulty and uncertainty of the future, the children never failed to amaze me with their thirst for knowledge and bright smiley faces and I really cherished my time with them. Nell, on the other hand, not only helped her father in the lighthouse but also helped the ladies in the village with their sewing. It was much more difficult to come by new material and cloth in these times so old items had to be mended and reused.

The three of us had been forced to grow up quickly. We saw things and we lost people that we shouldn't have. Our innocence of childhood had departed and we came to realise the utter importance of family, community and happiness but there were times when we just wanted to be children again and forget the recent heartbreaking and life-changing events.

We had been able to earn a little pocket money from our time helping, every now and then we would rather decadently, go for lunch together in The Beach Grotto. It really was an extravagance for us at the time to be able to spend the little money that we did have on having a meal out, something that could be taken for granted nowadays.

The Beach Grotto was decked out, as you would imagine, in a seaside style. The vast worn wooden panelled floors spread out to reach the jagged stone walls which also rather remarkably doubled up as the actual side of the cliff. These rock walls contained several nooks and crannies in which there were tables which housed small oil lamps. These shone in partnership with the other oil lamps dotted amongst the walls and hanging randomly between fishing nets and ship ornaments. I always loved the smell of the old oil burners against the wood, a mixture of rustic and industrial with a background tone of the salty sea air. The bar and kitchen were at the side of the entrance, making way for an open space in front of them which allowed for more tables who were offered a wonderful view of the patio area which overlooked the beach and the imposing Marsden Rock. We really were very lucky to have a place like this just on our doorstep.

The food served was predominantly fish-based and the beer on tap could only be Vaux, Sunderland's finest, which was brewed locally and shone like a half pint of golden honey. We always enjoyed going for lunch here but we were equally happy getting the Rattler to the town and eating proper local saveloys out of their waxy paper which crinkled in your hands as you ate.

Harry played in the village's football team. Nell and I would always go to watch him and the other men play against some of the rival mining villages. In those days there were no fancy stadiums or sports grounds and the matches were always played on the welfare field which belonged to the mine, a field where within a ninety-minute timeframe dreams could be made but also shattered. Nell and I were always very protective about Harry. I remember one of the miner's cup finals where there were some big brutes on the other team. These brutes had given Harry, who was playing up front, a right battering throughout and by the seventy-five-minute mark when Marsden were winning 1-0, one of them brought Harry down in a shockingly bad tackle. The spectators gasped and fell to a low hush apart from one loud lonesome shriek.

"Get off him." It was Nell. I had to physically hold her back before she went onto the pitch herself.

Harry was thankfully okay and got up and gave us a feeble wave. Nell turned to me and cunningly said, "I have had enough of those dirty tricks, well two can play that game."

And in a flash, she was gone and had run off to the lighthouse.

As the game re-commenced play, Harry had charge of the ball and was racing towards the opposition's goal when suddenly there was a mighty blast. The echoing boom of the foghorn crammed the air across the pitch, as the opposition jumped out of their skin and became disorientated, Harry fiercely kicked the ball into the back of the net making it 2-0 to Marsden. The final whistle blew and Marsden had succeeded and won the cup. Nell had resurfaced with a wicked smile on her face as she turned to me and said in a confident manner, "Bit of a sea fret there." I couldn't stop laughing. As our little community cheered and applauded, the team held Harry up on their shoulders like a hero but his eyes were fixated on only one person as he looked at her in worship, he was absolutely smitten with Nell Green.

That evening after the match, joy radiated out amongst the villagers and pretty much the whole village attended the monthly dance at the Miners' Welfare. A shabby stone building from the outside which had been weather-battered by the elements, it didn't look like much but inside was a different story. A warm and colourful entrance with Marsden Miners' banners adorning the walls, opened up to reveal a hall with a pool table in the corner and a small bar but the pièce de résistance was the second hall.

In the centre of the building was a ballroom, an arena with a heightened stage and an expansive shiny air sprung wooden dance floor which was lit up by a large chandelier. It felt like a magical place that looked quite out of place next to the sooty mine. We were all ready for a good knees-up that night to celebrate the cup coming to Marsden, the miners' band roared and the football team was treated like heroes. The whole room went dizzy with colour as men and ladies danced together using the whole length of the dance floor, their heavy boots pounding against the floor as they dashed from one end to the other in high rhythm.

Nell had her pick of men that night, she always did, but this night even more so due to her heroism with the foghorn and her part in the cup win. The whole team wanted to take her hand and dance with her and she happily obliged. I always felt bashful around men so I always danced with Harry. I felt comfortable with him as I knew he was my friend and wasn't interested in me in any other way: his heart belonged to Nell.

Harry and I would always have such a good time together but he would always cast a watchful eye on Nell, as did I. We didn't want her to get into any trouble if any of the other men, or equally women, grew jealous. Nell's innocence and desire to please everyone may have been perceived by others as being a tease. At the end of these evenings, Nell always made her way back to Harry and me, leaving a wake of broken hearts in her path. Harry would always deliver us safely home while we caught our breath back from all the dancing.

We spent our late teenage days mainly at the bay which lay at the foot of the village and we knew its beach like no one else at this point; all the intricate intertwining caves with all their privacy. We would spend many a day in those caves. We all still lived with our parents, so it was our own private little world. There was one cave in particular that we would go to and I remember it vividly. We had to climb a little way to reach it, carefully stepping through the shallow pools of collected sea water and rounded pebbles, to then find the partially concealed crevice which was the entrance to our private auditorium.

A flat smooth ledge and open space lay behind the opening and the limestone walls, so high that you could stand up in it and as wide as our house. Nell would bring one of the service lamps from the lighthouse and the whole cave would become illuminated and we could hear the gentle droplets of the North Sea trickling by from the small stream that lay below us. Harry and Nell had joined the miners' band a few years before; Harry as a trumpeter and Nell would sing. Nell always had the most unique voice, a rich deep tone which would have suited more of a jazz singer's voice. Harry would play jazz and Nell would sing: it was the only place they could practise whatever music they wanted where it would not disturb anyone in the village or the lighthouse. As soon as Nell opened her mouth to sing, Harry would just watch her in awe as the two of them melted into harmony together. I was not blessed with either of their musical talents, so I would often take my books to read but would be carried off into a velvet world of perfection. The acoustics in 'our' cave, paired with Nell's voice and Harry's sounds, were to me utter bliss.

It soon got to the point where we spent most of our time in the cave; it really was our retreat and a place we could call our own. We started to leave a collection of things in there, rather than carry them down all the time. Nell left the old service lamp hidden behind one of the rocks as it was no longer needed in the lighthouse and Harry often carried down supplies that we would leave in an old wicker basket under one of the splits in the rock. At any time, there were usually a few bottles of pop, bought weekly from the pop man in a variety of timeless flavours such as dandelion and burdock, sarsaparilla or lemonade, some of my books, some paper and pencils, biscuits and some blankets. The cave, rather surprisingly, always had a warmness about it, I think because of the concealed entrance there was never a draught in there and we used the blankets to sit on, as after all otherwise we would be sitting on bare rock face. Harry, without fail, would always lay the blankets out neatly for us before we sat down.

What I wouldn't give now to hear one more recital, sitting on one of the old woollen blankets, with a bottle of pop, in our cave, the scent of dry salty air filling my lungs to capacity as I inhaled the sound of Nell and Harry's sweet music.

LILY

December 1945

I t was New Year's Eve 1945 and everyone was looking forward to a new year to mark a new beginning. Nell, Harry and I decided we would all meet a few of our other friends and see the New Year in at The Beach Grotto. It was going to be a night to forget the past and to look ahead to the future, something which not only we needed but also the whole village and its surrounding community.

I had decided to go to the lighthouse to get ready with Nell; with the war firmly behind us now, we had grasped at the opportunity to buy some new dresses for the celebrations which Nell had intricately stitched to match the current fashion. I had bought a pillar-box red short sleeved floaty tea dress and Nell had bought a pale pastel blue one. We were both excited for the new year and had such fun getting ready together. We sat in Nell's compact and cosy room which overlooked the sea and took pleasure in doing each other's hair. Nell did mine first, carefully gathering strands of hair together and then she pinned my hair half up and half down with my auburn ringlets gently touching my shoulders.

"Lily, you look beautiful, the red really suits you. Let's put some rouge on your lips and some blush on your cheeks," said Nell excitedly.

We never ever had the chance to dress up like this, so I let Nell doll me up. I looked in the mirror and I was really pleased. I had never seen myself look like this before and I must admit, I felt quite lovely. Nell put on her dress and I put her white blonde hair into two intertwining plaits and pinned the hair up at the back; the style really suited her willowy frame. We finished off her make-up with a pink lip and a rosy-coloured cheek. Nell was always striking but tonight she looked incredible. We put our newly purchased and shined shoes on which Nell liked to describe as 'having a bit of a heel' and we waited excitedly for Harry to collect us.

The bell rang joyfully at the lighthouse cottage door; we knew it would be Harry. His dad had so kindly told the village that if we all got ready for half past six, he would get the Rattler out and take us all along to The Beach Grotto. It was not a long walk, about fifteen minutes in total, but in the cold winter weather and with everybody wanting to really celebrate the New Year, it was Mr Gunn's gift to us all. Nell ran upstairs to get our big winter coats and I opened the door.

"Oh Harry, you look so smart", I exclaimed as Harry leaned to kiss my cheek. Harry was wearing a suit with his dark wavy hair gelled over to one side, he must have really wanted to impress tonight as suits were hard to come by following the war.

"Lily, you look absolutely wonderful. It's going to be a night to remember. Where is Nell?" asked Harry.

Before I could answer, Nell swept down the staircase, coats in hand, in a cloud of perfume whilst Harry stared spellbound at her. I nudged Harry in the side and muttered to him, "Close your mouth Harry, it's rude to stare," whilst laughing heartily. Nell came up to us both with the coats and reached up to kiss Harry on the cheek. Harry took the coats and, ever the gentleman, helped me put my coat on and then went to help Nell. When Nell turned her back to him he mouthed at me 'I love her' and I mouthed back 'I know'. I had known for years, you would have had to be a fool not to notice.

We left the diminishing shine of the lighthouse behind us and linked arms with Harry, laughing together as we made our way to the Rattler whilst taking in deep breaths of the crisp winter air. Other members of the village joining us as we passed through from the lighthouse. We all got on the Rattler and made the short journey to The Beach Grotto, everybody singing and in high spirits. It was just what the village needed.

We decided to take the stairs down to the beach and let some of the elder people from the Rattler take it in turns to use the lift. We got to the beach after our descent and made our way with sunken footprints across the heavy sand to the pub which was welcomingly lit up and bustling with people. Now that we were eighteen we were officially able to have a few drinks in the pub and we were all really excited. We made our way into the entrance of the busy pub which had several members of the miners' band playing music spontaneously alongside the pub's record player. Suddenly on one side of the bar, we saw a wall of people, a vision of white; there were about thirty sailors in white uniforms. Where had they all come from? They all turned to look at us and we had all of these pairs of eyes staring at us.

I mumbled through gritted teeth to Nell, "They are all staring at you."

Nell replied, "Not just at me Lily, look at you."

We went to find a seat amongst some of our other friends from the village. We sat down, took our coats off and Harry very kindly got us all a perry. As I became accustomed to the busy surroundings of the pub, my eyes gazed across the bar and I became consumed with all of the happy faces of the pub goers. My eyes then drifted further until they were slowly lured into the sea of white. I thought to myself how handsome the sailors looked in their crisp white uniforms but also how very smart they were. As my eyes studied the faces that made up the group of sailors, it was then that I saw him.

A tall slim but muscular build which filled out his uniform, he was laughing heartily with the other sailors. I fixatedly couldn't remove my eyes off him. His hair, golden russet in colour, was gelled over to one side and his bright blue eyes glowed under the dim pub lights. He turned to look at me and smiled, the best smile I had ever seen. Time appeared to stand still, my heart raced and my tummy had butterflies. I boldly found myself smiling back and he started to walk over towards me.

He reached for my hand in a gentlemanly way. I daringly let him take it and he politely kissed it.

"Hello," he said in a deep crisp voice. "May I have the pleasure of buying you another drink?"

I didn't know what to say. I had never let a man buy me a drink before but before I could think, Nell had kicked me under the table and replied to the man, "Yes she would love another perry, wouldn't you, Lily?"

The man smiled at me again and said, "Lily. What a beautiful name. I will get you a perry and then come back if that's okay with you?" I nodded.

The man went back to the bar and Nell nudged me again and giggled. Harry looked more cautious and moved round closer to Nell and made some space next to me for when the man returned.

The man sat beside me and I thanked him for the drink and carefully took a sip of my offering.

"Nice to meet you, Lily. I am Thom but everyone calls me Red."

I quickly learned that Red and his fellow sailors had all been active and stationed in the war. They were now all, thankfully, back home in the South Shields area and those who did not already have families had decided to spend New Year's Eve together. They had decided to pick The Beach Grotto as it overlooked the sea which I thought was a very noble decision from them. Red was from Harton, just up the road from Marsden. I could not believe that I had grown up just a few miles away from this incredible man. There was an instant connection between Red and me: we talked about our families, our aspirations for the future, his time at sea and he met my Nell and Harry. After another few perrys, a few of the miners' started up playing again along with the music. The whole pub started to dance and was in a raucous joy. Nell was up with Harry; the men stamped their feet to the music and spun their ladies. Red took me in his arms and we danced and laughed and spun in such a manner that there was no way of knowing where he ended and I began.

Suddenly, there was a bit of a commotion next to us, I looked down and there was Nell on the floor laughing heartily with Harry by her side who was looking a bit embarrassed. Nell's heel on her shoe had snapped in two, causing the pair of them to fall over. They sat the next few dances out rather than Nell dance barefoot or with only one shoe on, not that this would have stopped her, but Harry insisted in case her foot was trodden on. Harry came over to me and said he had offered to take Nell home to see in the New Year at the lighthouse. He wanted to check that I would be able to get back home okay with the others on the Rattler. He hugged me close and whispered in my ear.

"Happy New Year, Lily, here's to a great year. I am going to tell Nell how I feel tonight." I hugged him back tightly and kissed him lovingly on the cheek, showing my approval. I went and said my goodbyes to Nell and then watched them head off, with ever-the-gentleman Harry giving Nell a piggy back to the lift.

I stayed with Red for the rest of the evening. It was getting near to midnight and the landlord announced he was putting a slower song on for the lead up to the new year, the opening bars of 'My Romance' filled the midnight air and Red pulled me in tightly and gently held me against him as we swayed to the music. I could just have stayed there like that in that moment forever. At the end of the song, the countdown for the New Year had begun; everybody raced out the doors and onto the freezing sand and began counting down from ten. Red and I joined in. I don't know if it was the promise of a new year, the happiness on everyone's faces or the few glasses of perry but at the stroke of midnight, I embraced Red and kissed him on the lips.

He then softly whispered in my ear "Happy New Year, Lily. The start of something wonderful."

We all then crazily ran about the sand and dipped our toes in the icy cold North Sea. As I took Red's hand to go back inside, I looked up at the lighthouse, something I always did when I was on the beach. In the dark shadow of night, the lighthouse majestically stood out with its beacon of light. As I looked up to the top of the lighthouse I could see a dark shape. I squinted my eyes to try and see more clearly: I could make out two figures now and they were intertwined; it was Harry and Nell and they were kissing. Harry must have finally told her how he felt and Nell must have felt the same way. I could not wait to hear all about it.

When we got back into The Beach Grotto, Mr Colman, the landlord, had brought out a keg of Vaux free of charge for everyone which really elevated the celebrations. I spent the rest of the evening with Red and we danced together joyfully to the last few songs. We all started to get ready to get back on the Rattler and back to the village. When I came to say goodbye to Red, I didn't want to leave him. How could I when I had only just found him?

"Lily, I will come by for you tomorrow," whispered Red as he gallantly helped me onto the Rattler.

"I really cannot wait," I whispered back to him.

I waved Red off and got back safely to my house. I greeted my mam and dad who had been celebrating together at home and went up to my childhood room in a trance-like state with a giddy smile on my face. As I lay on my bed I thought about this delightful night. I didn't want it to end, it had been like someone else's dream. I thought about Red over and over, I absorbed his perfect face, his muscular stature, his deep voice, his woody smell, his protective frame...

Until the room went dark and I must have eventually drifted off.

LILY

January 1946

I was woken up by the sizzling smell of fried bacon wafting up the staircase and the sound of my mam happily humming along to the wireless. I stretched out my body and I smiled to myself when I remembered him and the most flawless evening I had experienced the night before. I couldn't wait to be reacquainted with him again. Then I remembered Nell and Harry; I couldn't wait to find out what had happened with them either. I threw on my old worn dressing gown and went downstairs, where my dad had his arms affectionately wrapped around my mam and they were swaying together to the music as she cooked the bacon. If I could have somebody love me and look at me the way my dad did to my mam, I would be happy in life.

"Good Morning," I said brightly as I sat down at the little old wooden table in the kitchen. My mam and dad turned around simultaneously and smiled at me.

"Good Morning Lily," said my mam, who was wearing her cooking pinny. "Do you want a cup of tea? Did you have a lovely new year with Nell and Harry?"

I was grinning from ear to ear. I didn't want to tell my parents about Red just yet, so I said I had a wonderful evening. I guzzled down my bacon and hot cup of tea as I couldn't wait to get over to the lighthouse to see Nell. I hurriedly put some clothes on, yelled bye to mam and dad, sneaked out into the back lane (as I dared not run into Harry before I had seen Nell) and I ran over to the lighthouse. Nell must have been as excited as I was as she was loitering near the door for me when I got there. We gave each other a huge hug and scrambled up the stairs into the safety of her bedroom.

"So," said Nell intriguingly, "Tell me."

I proceeded to detail for Nell the evening's events after she and Harry had left.

"I am smitten Nell, he is just perfect and he is such a gentleman. I have never met anyone like him before, I long for him and I only saw him ten hours ago. I hope he didn't get the wrong idea about me as I kissed him on the lips at midnight, the excitement just took control of me."

"He said he would come to the Village today to see me, I can't wait to see him again."

Nell grinned at me and agreed that Red was ruggedly attractive and that together we made a very beautiful couple.

45

"Anyhow," I said, "Tell me Nell, what happened with you and Harry? Harry went to some real effort and looked incredibly handsome last night."

Nell blushed and giggled, I had never seen her look so shy. I took her hand and giggled too and Nell told me what happened.

"After we left the party, Harry practically carried me back to the lighthouse. My parents were in the cottage so we decided we would see the New Year in together in the lighthouse in private whilst looking out at the sea. We took up a small bottle of perry, two glasses and a blanket. At the top of the lighthouse we just sat together with my head lying on Harry's chest. As I looked out into the sea with the low light shining on Harry, I suddenly realised something, I didn't want to be anywhere else or with anyone else."

Nell giggled again and I urged her to continue.
"As it got nearer midnight I decided I would kiss him and see what he would do, hoping he would not be horrified by it." By this point I was beaming at Nell, having known how Harry felt about her.

"As midnight approached we filled our glasses ready to toast the new year in. We started the countdown and at midnight I said, 'Happy New Year, Harry' and I went in for the kiss. Harry stopped me, he put his finger on my lips and said 'Wait'. He then said to me 'Nell, I have been building up to tell you this all evening and I want to say this first, you are the love of my life. I have loved you from the first moment I met you and my love for you will never fade. Will you give us a try at being together?'

I beamed at Nell. "What did you say to him, Nell?"

Nell then continued rather confidently, "I placed my fingers behind his head, brought him close to me and whispered, 'There is no other person I would rather be with'. I then kissed him properly and we embraced again and again until we both fell asleep in each other's arms."

Nell added giddily, "Lily, we are a couple now, me and Harry. Can you believe it after all these years?"

I hugged Nell close and was so incredibly happy for her and Harry. My two best friends together at last. I had always known that this day would come and I was so pleased it had happened at the same time I had met Red. What a year we would have together!

Our secret chat was then disturbed by a noise outside the lighthouse herb garden and the next thing we heard was a knock on the lighthouse cottage door. Nell went to answer it and it was Harry, there was somebody else with him.

"Look who I found walking through the village," said Harry. It was Red. My heart skipped a beat when I saw that charming smile once again but I also felt nervous to see him.

We were going to go to the tea rooms in Binns in the town but we soon foolishly realised that nothing would be open with it being New Year's Day. Instead, we sat in the parlour room at the lighthouse and had a pot of tea. It was like I had known Red forever; there was no awkwardness and we all just chatted together at ease. As it reached afternoon, I thought we should leave Nell and Harry to be alone together as they had only just become a pair. I said to Red, "How about we walk along the beach and take in the crisp New Year's Day air?" Red thought that would be lovely.

Even though Red was only from Harton which was not far from Marsden, he had never really been to Marsden beach, instead always favouring South Shields. We walked to the stairs next to The Beach Grotto and we took each step carefully as Red held my hand, and to my delight he didn't let go once we reached the last step. We then walked along the beach hand in hand, it just felt so very natural. Suddenly it started to drizzle and then the heavens opened; you can never trust the North East weather. Red tried to give me his coat but I pulled his hand and shouted, "Come on," as I led him towards the cliffs and the darkened entrance to our secret cave.

We got into the access to the cave and I pulled him up to the concealed entrance of mine, Harry and Nell's hideaway. As we got into the ledge he must have wondered what on earth I was doing in near darkness, as I scrambled, rather ungracefully, behind another ledge to pull out the old service lamp from the lighthouse along with a woollen blanket. I switched the lamp on and suddenly the hidden part of the cave shone brightly, the jutting edges of the rock illuminated with the soft sashaying of water lapping in the distance. Red could not believe how warm and dry it was in this part of the cave. I spread the blanket out on the flat crevice, popped open two bottles of lemonade that were also in our stash and motioned for Red to come and sit beside me.

"What else have you got in here?" laughed Red. "I have never seen anything like it and I have seen things as a sailor!"

We sat next to each other and reminisced about our wonderful evening, laughing about Nell's shoe, the cheerful dancing and the sound of laughter and joy that was radiating from each and every person in that room. Red then took my hand and looked more serious.

"Lily, I can't stop thinking about you," he whispered nervously. I knew I was blushing at this point. "You took my breath away last night as soon as you looked at me, I knew I had to get to know you."

It was funny as I had thought the same thing about him; there was something about him that drew me to him.

"'Not only are you beautiful, Lily," Red continued, "but you are clever, elegant and also independent. I really admire that, do you think that we could perhaps start courting?"

I was so pleased, I was hoping we might have talked about this today but didn't really believe it would happen to me, it was what I really wanted. I said a bashful 'yes' to

Red. Red then gently took his hand to my face and brought my mouth to his and we kissed properly. I couldn't think of a more fitting special place to have my first proper kiss with Red.

We stayed in the cave for a little longer, laughing some more, chatting some more about his time as a sailor and how he was looking for new work and stealing a few more secret kisses. After we had cleared everything away we got back to the entrance and it was already starting to get dark outside. We must have been in there for a few hours. I found that time passed quickly when I was with Red. We made our way up the steep whitewashed stairs and Red walked me back to the village and I showed him my house in the little line of terraces. The dusk was creeping in from the sea now and only a few solitary lamps lit the village green. I pulled Red into the back lane of the street and we hid ourselves from the outside, our silhouettes masked by the shadows.

"I can't wait to see you again," I said as he held me closely. I could feel his breath on my neck.

Red whispered, "I will come back again tomorrow and every day after."

I already couldn't wait. "You will be able to get the Rattler tomorrow and not have to walk in the winter's air," I said cheerfully. "Come to the house mid-morning, I will tell my mam and dad about you tonight and they will want to meet you."

Red lifted his head, smiled, nodded and then leaned in for one final kiss under the shadow of darkness, my heart pounding relentlessly as I waved him off and sneaked round from the back lane to the front door.

Following my uncharacteristic deception, I was greeted inside the terrace by my mam and dad. I sat with them in the cosy little kitchen as my mam made me a cup of tea to warm me up.

"Lily, you look somehow different today," remarked my mam, (how do mams always know about everything?). "You look so very happy, your face is glowing."

I knew I would be able to pretend it was just from coming in from the cold air outside to our warm and snug house, but I knew my mam would not believe just that.

"Well actually I am very happy, Mam. I met someone. I have never met anyone like him before."

My mam smiled whereas my dad coughed unexpectedly. I quickly explained to them both about Thom, how he was from Harton, how he had completed his marine engineering exams before he ended up being active in the latter parts of the war, how he was five years older than me, how he was looking for new work now that he was home and how everyone called him Red.

"Slow down, Lily!" laughed my mam, who could clearly tell I was besotted with Red.

My dad shrugged his shoulders and said, "Well Lily, I would like to meet him."

I explained to my dad that I knew he would, so I thought it would be good for Red to come to the house tomorrow. Dad nodded. I thought that he would always see me as a little girl even though I was now a grown woman. I went to bed again that night already looking forward to what the new day would bring.

The morning passed endlessly slow, until at half past ten there was a knock on the front door. My heart flipped; I knew it would be Red. I went to open the door to let him in so that he could meet my parents. I could see his frame through the glass in the door. I creaked open the old door and there Red stood, smart as anything holding some rock scones for my mam and dad to enjoy with our cup of tea. We all sat down in the little kitchen where mam had set out the wooden table ready for his arrival. Red greeted my parents and, what can I say, for the next two hours he charmed them. My parents learned about his family, his work and his time at sea, so much so that my dad invited Red to stay for lunch. My mam got a bit flustered, as with it having just been Christmas and New Year the butchers had not yet opened so instead of posh meat sandwiches, as my mam called them and which she would have preferred to have made for a special occasion, she served corned beef ones. Red said they would be perfect and one of his favourites and how he would much prefer them to anything else and we all just laughed together. I was so

relieved and pleased that mam and dad liked Red. I don't
know what I would have done if they had not approved.

For the next three months I saw Red every day; our lives
had become one life together. We did the usual things that
our generation did in this time such as eat together, drink
together, play games together and go to the regal old
cinema in South Shields. I used to love the cinema; it was a
chance to escape into a different world, a fantasy and to
become enveloped in other people's lives and
circumstances. I remember being entranced by the
glamour of the proper Hollywood films and the elegance
and classiness of the leading ladies. They were truly
magnificent with their beautiful lace and silk dresses,
ebony lined eyes and deep red lips, I was only a young girl
from a small miner's village but I vowed that one day I
would be as glamorous as them. A lot of our cinema and
general outings obviously involved Harry and Nell and to
my utter joy, our trio became a quartet.

Red had continued to look for work and one quiet dreary
day he got the news he was hoping for. Red had been
successful at interview and was due to start a job working
in the shipyard in South Shields. He was going to assist on
the engineering side of a cargo ship currently being built,
and after that he would be one of the engineers who would
be posted aboard the ship to deliver it to its new owners.
The new owners were in Brazil, so it would mean my Red

would be away for six months. I didn't know how I would survive without him but I knew it was too good an opportunity for him to turn down. We knew we would have to make the most of the next three months together before he went to sea and we lived for those last weekends together.

I remember one of those weekend outings vividly. Spring had sprung and the four of us went to the nearby Whitburn Park, where there was to be a gala to celebrate the community and the Marsden miners' band were performing. Nell and Harry were part of the band and we marched alongside them as we heard the oompahs from the brass and Nell striking the cymbals. Once they reached the bandstand, the atmosphere changed into a celebratory one and Nell was able to sing, her dusky tones belting out some of the current hits alongside some old favourites. When she started to sing 'My Bonnie Lies over the Ocean' against the strong and rich sounds of the brass band, I held Red close to me and I just wanted to sob.

"Come on Lily, let's go for a walk," Red said as he took my hand to lead me around the familiar local park. As we weaved in and out of the dancing smiling faces of the daffodils and crocuses in the flower beds, we came upon a quiet bench hidden behind the trees at the back of the park. We sat on the bench and Red took my hands gently in his and he turned to face me.

"Lily, I have been wanting to say this for a while now." Red lovingly clutched my hands and looked me directly in the eyes and softly said, "I love you."

I smiled with a sparkle in my eyes as I savoured those significant words and I eagerly said the same back to Red.

He then replied with, "You mustn't worry whilst I am away, the job will help us to build our future together."

Deep down, I did know this, but it still pained me to think I would be apart from my love for so long.

ANNA

February 2017

It was a longed for but standard Friday evening after a full and busy week at work. James and I had ordered a take away and were planning to have a quiet night in. As we cuddled up together on our worn and sunken crinkly brown sofa, which had become imprinted with our joint outline, I reached out to pour some of our favourite jerk sauce over our tasty bucket of chicken ready to watch one of our much-loved films and I suddenly had a realisation.

"James, I just love being like this," I said happily.

James turned to me and viewed me quizzically with a raised eyebrow and replied, "What do you mean Anna?"

I responded with, "Like this! Just comfortable and relaxed with you and eating really yummy food. This is what I want people to feel like at our wedding, it's us."

James laughed and joked, "And we could serve jerk chicken to our guests and tell them to wear their pyjamas!"

I smiled back at James who was still laughing. "Seriously though James, I just want a nice relaxed wedding with good food. I think you have something there with the idea about the chicken though, why don't we get married in the Caribbean? We did actually meet each other while we were gorging on Caribbean food."

James's eyes slowly lit up as I could tell he was processing the idea.

"Just think, James," I continued, "we could have the music, the food, the sun and such a mellow atmosphere: it could be just perfect."

As I thought about it more, I really liked the notion of a Caribbean wedding and James and I agreed that we would seriously think about having our wedding out there, as long as our families would be able to attend and that we would start to do some research on a wedding abroad.

I was due to have a lunch catch up my friends in Newcastle and I was eager and looking forward to sharing my Caribbean plans with them but I still felt quite hurt about Nora's comments about my ring and couldn't put it to the back of my mind properly. I kept just trying to blame it on her being drunk. As I got on the Metro to travel into the city, I started to feel quite nervous about seeing Nora. I hadn't really spoken to her since our engagement party and I wondered if she might apologise for her bitchy words.

I disembarked the Metro, which was running late and meandered up the silver metallic conveyer belt to reach the mouth of the station which streamed out onto Grey Street with its ornate Georgian architectural facades and subtle ladylike curve. I made my way down the bend and to the entrance of the beautifully regal former bank which now housed one of my favourite bars. I took a deep breath and made my way in.

In the corner of the plush seating area with pride of place at the head of the leather-bound table was Nora who was commanding the attention of our other three friends by gesticulating her arms about her body, whilst giggling over her prosecco glass.

As her eyes met mine she raised her glass and bellowed, "Anna, you made it. Come and get a glass."

I sat down and greeted our other mutual friends, Zoe, Kate and Jo, who all beamed at me and started to congratulate me on mine and James's engagement as they all cooed over my ring.

"How exquisite," remarked Jo as she looked deeply into the rich blue flash of the sapphire. "James really is so thoughtful to pick you a ring which is your birthstone."

I nodded and smiled as the others fawned over the proposal and how it was so romantic, my mood was lowered however as I could feel a pair of eyes burning on me.

Nora was glaring at me then lifted her glass again and slurred, "I like classic best, mind. A nice solitaire diamond but everyone has different tastes," as she then tried to laugh and make light of her stinging comment.

The tension was then dispersed by the cheery waitress who came over to take our lunch orders. At that point, it then became very clear why Nora was so drunk so quickly.

"I will take the chicken salad but no croutons, no dressing, no extras, just plain," requested Nora, in between a hiccup. "I have a wedding to plan for and a dress to fit into," she added matter-of-factly to the waitress who just wanted to write down the order quickly.

I ordered the cheeseburger.

The discussion then turned to the topic of Nora's wedding. "Have you found a venue yet?" asked Jo.

Nora then went through in detail how her and her fiancé, Tim, had just finalised their contract with the exclusive Sinton Hall in London. Tim, whom Nora had met eighteen months ago, came from an extremely wealthy family and no expense was being spared on the wedding, a fact which Nora was fond of repeating. The three girls and I sat and listened incredulously at the lengthening list of Nora's wedding plans. She planned to wear a designer dress ('a steal at £8k for such high quality craftmanship'), there would be a midnight firework display ('who doesn't have fireworks these days, really'), a seven tiered hand-painted cake had been selected at one of London's finest bakeries ('the painted pictures give the cake something extra'), guests would be treated to various keepsakes which would include a personalised bottle of champagne, a charm bracelet for the ladies and cufflinks for the men ('Tim and I know what people expect these days'), the list went on and on and on. I couldn't help myself, I sat open-mouthed. I couldn't believe how much Nora was changing before my eyes. The wedding had really taken a hold of her and she was being swept away by it.

"Why have you picked to have the wedding in London?" I asked.

Nora snapped back with a raised eyebrow, "Where else would we have it? It's not like there is anywhere up here which could hold our wedding."

I was quite shocked by her reply. Nora's grandparents and her great aunt were quite elderly now and there was no way they would be able to make the journey to London. I felt very sad for them and I said, "But what about your Aunt Ida and your Nanna and Pops?"

Nora rolled her eyes and said sharply, 'They can't come, we talked it through with them and it's for the best. They understand we want to get married in London."

I didn't know what to say at that point, and as the conversation continued, it also became clear, that Nora would be inviting no children to her wedding, a fact I couldn't get my head round either, given the number of children in her family. I started to feel really upset for her family and how it would affect them. This was a girl I had known all my life and had grown up with, but at that moment I felt like I barely even recognised her.

After we had eaten, Zoe ordered another bottle of prosecco and poured everyone a glass.

"Anna, have you and James thought much about your wedding yet?" the girls enquired.

I sipped my drink and then said, "Actually, we have had a bit of a think and we have an idea, we are looking towards a venue in the Caribbean for a beachy sort of wedding in the sun. We know we don't want a huge wedding and thought something like that might be nice."

Zoe, Jo and Kate all nodded with encouragement which was then followed by a tut from the other side of the table.

"The Caribbean? Will there not be loads of flies and dirt there and the food is not very advanced is it?" said Nora rather narrow-mindedly.

"Actually, the venues we have been looking at are all lovely," I responded rather curtly, before deciding to not say anything further about it. There was no point in arguing with Nora who was obviously in a funny mood and especially in front of our other friends who looked embarrassed by her outburst.

We all went our separate ways after that last drink, and after what I can only describe as an awkward lunch encounter. I got back on the Metro and sat quietly seething the entire forty minutes from Monument to Seaburn. By the time I reached Seaburn, I had revisited the lunch conversation several times until I had reached boiling point. I was furious and so hot and bothered I could imagine the steam piping out of my ears. James picked me up from the station and as soon as I got in the car he could recognise my fury without me uttering a single word, "Anna, what on earth is the matter?"

I had an eruption as I began to tell James about some of the things which Nora had said and how they had upset me and about some of her ambitious plans for her wedding. When I got to the part explaining the virtual racing games, James just laughed, which angered me more but then I had to laugh too when I realised how silly and unnecessary some of the things Nora was going to have at her wedding were and how she was really missing the point a bit.

At our house I hugged James, calmed down and relaxed into his welcoming arms. I always felt like everything in the world would be okay when I was smothered in those arms; he made me see things from a sensible point of view.

That night I lay awake on our bed. I couldn't sleep properly and my mind raced. I kept going over some of Nora's words but the flashes of images that kept repeating in my mind were not of words but of faces, faces which I knew. Firstly, of the tear-streaked faces of Nora's Auntie Ida, Nanna and Pops who couldn't attend the wedding of the little girl they loved deeply and had nurtured into adulthood; these faces would then become juxtaposed with a face I knew very well, the precious face of my own gran. I suddenly became haunted by the face of my beautiful gran with those deep dark eyes weeping and sitting in a room on her own, torturing herself when trying to understand why she was not attending her own much-loved granddaughter's wedding. I jerked and sat bolt upright, sweat dripping distastefully down my back, as James calmly held my face.

"Anna, Anna, it's okay, you are having a nightmare?" James stated concerningly.

I looked at James, gained lucidness again and broke down in tears.

"I can't not have my gran at our wedding," I muttered between sobs.

James held me close. "There is no way we would exclude people, Anna. We said that from the beginning, don't worry."

I managed to somehow get back to sleep and in the morning, things became a lot clearer. I needed to see my gran so I went to visit her and explained some of Nora's strange behaviour to her.

"Try not to take it personally, Anna," my gran encouraged. "Weddings sometimes do strange things to people and they don't realise how their actions might have an impact on others."

I reflected on my wise gran's advice and I nodded. "Some more so than others," I chuckled.

We sat there together in her peaceful, floral garden looking out to the openness of the sea and I forgot about Nora and wanted to talk to my gran about something else, something which had sparked a deep interest in me.

I turned to her, saying, "Gran, tell me more about the village and what happened back then, if you don't mind please?"

I then waited as my gran made herself comfortable and we sat in her tranquil garden that afternoon and drifted back into her past and into another lifetime.

LILY

April 1946

I t was April now, spring was beckoning and Red and I
had only a few months left together before he went off
to sea. Life in the village continued. I had been offered a
part-time job to help to support the children in the local
school which I was delighted to accept. The headmistress
said she had really valued my assistance during the war
and wanted to keep me there. I would keep myself busy
during the week by working at the school three mornings
and by helping my mam with her daily chores. Nell
continued to help with the lighthouse and her dad had
given both her and Harry proper apprenticeships to work
alongside him. Nell was especially delighted as she got to
learn a new trade and spend her day at work with Harry by
her side. Red would work at the shipyard during the week
often doing long hours. I still managed to see him every
evening, even though he must have been very tired; time
was precious for us. Red felt like part of the family now
and I felt like part of his. We would always try to spend as

much of the weekend together as we could and spend time with Nell and Harry. There is one weekend that will live with me forever and it is one I will never forget.

I had woken up early on the Saturday morning by birds singing! We hardly ever got song birds in the village with it being so near to the sea, their sweet sound signalling the dawn of a new season. The four of us had decided to treat ourselves to celebrate our new jobs and we wanted to go to The Beach Grotto for lunch. I felt ever so grown up. Nell and Harry said they would meet us there as Nell wanted to check around the big rock for any fallen seabirds. I decided to wear my red dress from New Year again as it seemed like such a glorious day outside. I pinned my hair back a little and put on some red lipstick as I was now an independent lady with my own wage. I spritzed some of my Lily of the Valley perfume and stepped forward, spinning myself around in the scented air before I went downstairs. Red was coming to the house for ten a.m. and would have some tea with my parents before we met Nell and Harry. My mam put the tea kettle on the stove which whistled as it heated the water and Red arrived, true to his word, at ten a.m. on the dot. We all had nice cups of tea and a bit of a chat, before my mam and dad gathered their things together as they were going to go to the town and mam wanted to get there before Saturday market closed. We waved my parents off and Red took my hand, flashed me a cheeky smile and kissed it.

"You look exceptionally beautiful today," he said. It made me giggle as I held his hand back.

We locked up the little old terrace, my childhood home, and made our way down the gravelly path and out of the village and down the grassy covered dunes to those old faithful whitewashed stairs. As we carefully scaled the steps to the beach, the midnight blue sea glistened in the April sun, with the crisp white tufty heads of the seabirds bobbing up and down in rhythm with the gentle waves. I took in a deep breath of the fresh salty sea air as we made our way to the final step. We crossed the sand hand-in-hand before Red and I entered The Beach Grotto where Nell and Harry had already got us one of the cosy tables in one of The Beach Grotto's caves. We all sat together around the little wooden table with The Beach Grotto's delicate oil lamps lighting the scene. We ordered some drinks and perused the cardboard menu. As it was such a nice mild day outside we all picked the battered fish pieces and fried potatoes and heartily tucked in. As we all sat full to capacity from our over-eating, Harry looked deep in thought before he smiled at us all.

"Who would have thought it?" remarked Harry. "Here we all are with new jobs and looking forward to the future, let's do a toast to this very moment and to the future."

We all clinked our glasses together as Harry winked at me.

Red took my hand then and said, "'Lily, let's go for a wander along the beach and take in some of the sea air to help us digest."

I gladly took his hand and asked Harry and Nell if they wanted to come too. Nell shook her head vigorously and said she was too full and just wanted to sit a little while longer.

Red and I left The Beach Grotto behind and walked down the grey stone steps and onto the golden sand. We walked across the sand to the point where it began to sink beneath our feet. As we reached the water's edge we removed our shoes and let the tide gently lap over our toes. As we strolled further along the sand we left footprints to mark our path. When we got to the other side of the beach Red took my arm and twirled me round to face him.

"I love you so much Lil, you do know that don't you?" Red asked tenderly. I smiled and nodded happily at him, as he kissed me and we gently danced barefoot in the sand together for a few moments, my red dress fluttering in the fresh sea breeze; a few moments that I never wanted to end.

We put our shoes back on to get ourselves ready to walk back along the dry part of the sand which was nearer the caves. As we tiptoed over the sand carefully avoiding the many pebbles, Red suddenly remarked, "Oh Lily, I remember, I left my hat in the cave last week, can we just go in and get it?"

I shrugged as I could not remember a hat and thought we should be getting back to Harry and Nell.

"Okay" I said. "But let's be quick."

Red led me into the darkness of our cave and as we made our way along to the ledge ready to go into the secret hideaway, I noticed a change, something felt different. The cave had a dim light. I wondered if Nell and Harry were somehow already in our cave.

As we slowly climbed up and over the ledge and turned our bodies to stand up straight, it took a minute for my eyes to become accustomed to the change in the light and I could not believe what I saw.

In our cave, the place where Red and I had our first proper kiss and which had been such a fundamental part of my childhood, there were about twenty-five small oil lamps which were lit and which were illuminating the cave in its full glory. The flecks of limestone in the walls twinkled and the small droplets of water which clung to the edge of each gentle spike shone like tiny diamonds. In the middle of the lamps was a carefully placed blanket which was surrounded by daffodils, their little heads smiling gleefully at me and inviting me to come over to the blanket which also had placed on it a small bottle of sparkling wine with two glasses.

My heart began to race as Red took my hand and smiled at me coyly, "Come and sit with me, Lily," said Red as he led me to the blanket.

As I approached the blanket, Red let go of my hand and twirled me again to face him. He then gradually bent down until he was at the point where he was on one knee and in his hand was a little brown box with some gold letters on it, the most wonderful little box I had ever seen in my life. I gasped and looked at him wide-eyed, I dared not to believe what he would say next.

Red looked nervous. I could see his hand was shaking as he held the small box tightly. His voice trembled as he uttered the most beautiful words I could imagine.

"Lily, love of my life, my entire life, would you do me the greatest honour of marrying me?"

Red opened the little brown box to reveal its contents and inside was the loveliest ring, a silver ring with a larger diamond in the middle and then six little diamonds on either side to encase the band. Red took the ring carefully out of the box which made the diamonds catch the light and gleam under the glow of the oil lamps. I knelt down on the blanket to match Red's kneeling height as he patiently awaited my response. I placed my hand behind his head and pulled his mouth towards mine as I kissed him passionately.

I then said excitedly, "Yes, Red, of course I will marry you."

Red placed the ring onto my finger, my ring, as he opened the little bottle of wine and popped the cork which echoed throughout the cave. As we sipped the bubbly wine which I had never tasted before, I couldn't believe I was now engaged and to my Red.

"Thank you," I said graciously as I held Red tightly.

Red responded, "For what Lily?"

"For this," I said as I motioned my arm towards the cave.

"This is just so special and so thoughtful. I love you so much, Red and I can't wait until I can be your wife."

We finished the sparkling wine off, enjoying every bubbly morsel of it, dimmed the oil lamps and I gathered up the joyful daffodils to take back with me. I couldn't wait to tell my parents our happy news and of course, Nell and Harry. I was so elated.

"Come on," said Red. "Let's go back to The Beach Grotto and celebrate."

I nodded but explained to Red that I wanted to tell our parents the news first before we told anyone else, even Nell and Harry. We strode giddily back towards The Beach Grotto and made our way into the friendly pub. Red never failed to surprise me; he had planned the whole proposal to the last detail. Six pairs of eyes stared at us as we came through the door and then all eyes fixated sharply on my finger, in a table in the corner sat my mam and dad, Red's mam and dad and Nell and Harry. Nell was first to jump up. She ran over and hugged us both, followed by everyone else. There were lots of congratulations, pats on backs and showing of my ring. My dad then ordered us all some sparkling perry. It transpired that Red had asked my dad for his permission for my hand in marriage earlier in the month, so my mam and dad knew about the proposal. Nell and Harry had also played a part, in that they had quickly lit all the lamps and done a final check of the cave whilst Red and I were walking along the beach. I really felt quite moved by their collusion to make the proposal just as Red wanted it for me.

We rejoiced, ate, and drank in The Beach Grotto until the early evening with lots of laughing and talking of the future. As we all went to head home, our parents hugged and went off on their separate ways and Nell and Harry headed back to the lighthouse. The evening was still light, so Red and I went to the grassy area near the cliff edge to sit together and to look out at the sea. I placed my head on Red's shoulder and took a deep breath, taking in everything that had happened in the day as well as the scent of the sea air mixed with Red's woody aftershave. As I thought about the future, our future, I knew I was certain of one thing.

"Red," I whispered, "I want to be your wife before you need to go away."

Red's eyes looked at me with pride.

"I couldn't think of anything I would want more, either," he said approvingly, as he wrapped his jacket around my shoulders to protect me from the cooler evening air and held me in towards him tightly. We looked out at the never-ending blue backdrop that lay in front of us and knew it was like the start of our future together, a perfect unspoilt prospect, deep down another part of me became panicky as I also knew it was the very thing which would keep us apart.

LILY

May 1946

For the next few weeks we were awash with plans for the wedding and also attempting to try and buy our first house together. We knew we wanted to marry in May, so it left us little time to make plans for both. One of the first things we decided together as a couple was to involve Harry and Nell as part of the wedding. There was never any question that Nell would be my bridesmaid and Red asked Harry to be his best man, something which deeply moved me as he knew just how much Harry meant to me and I was delighted that Red and Harry had also developed a deep bond.

The marriage was to take place in the cosy church which we had visited since we were little and there was only one place where we knew we wanted to hold the celebrations after the marriage and that was The Beach Grotto.

Nell came over to the terrace excitedly one early May morning as she wanted to discuss everything to do with the dresses.

"Lily, I still can't believe you will be married in a few weeks, are you starting to feel nervous? Surely you must be now?"

In all honesty, I wasn't. From the moment I met Red, I knew there was something about him and I couldn't help feeling like he had been intended for me. I really could not wait to become his wife.

"Have you thought much about your dress?" enquired Nell chirpily.

"Well, there are some things I think I would like but I think I would need to look at the dresses in more detail," I replied, giggling.

We decided without delay that we would go into the town to start to look at wedding dresses and also to get a dress for Nell to be bridesmaid. My mam grabbed her coat as she was eager to join us. As we all hurried out the door and down to get the Rattler we cheerfully talked more about the wedding. I explained that I would like white roses as my flowers and I would like Nell to wear a blue dress. For the reception Red and I knew that we would like prawns as a starter and then a beef roast dinner followed by our wedding cake. I told Nell we wanted the miners' band to play at the wedding.

"Oh," I gasped suddenly, "Red and I will have to pick a song for our first dance. We don't have a song."

I didn't think any more about it as the Rattler came to a halt in the town. Nell, my mam and I skipped down the old stone cobbled street and into Tulips which was the bridal shop. I enthusiastically tried on a few dresses which I really enjoyed and thought were nice but not quite right for me but then I looked over to the corner of the smart shop and saw it. A white full skirt which was nipped in at the waist with a v-shaped neckline, tight bodice, and guipure lace sleeves. It was exquisite. It was like a film star dress. I really hoped it could be my film star dress and I immediately wanted to try it on. As I came out of the little changing room, dressed head to toe in white, I saw my mam and Nell's expressions change.

Nell's voice stammered, which was unusual for her. "Lily, you look utterly breath-taking," she said as her eyes welled up.

My mam just looked at me with sheer pride. I looked in the mirror and I was shocked, I didn't recognise myself. The figure staring back at me was one of a woman, a very beautiful woman who looked like a bride. My mam agreed the sale with the Tulips lady there and then and suddenly the wedding felt real.

Nell took me to one side. "Lily, as a gift to you please could I make your veil?"

I was very touched by Nell's gesture and kindly accepted it.

We then made the way across town to Binns to look for a dress for Nell but stopped at the little café in Binns first to have some lunch. I always loved it in Binns with its high glass chandeliers, sweet scents, white linen and stainless silver cutlery; it really did make me feel like royalty. We managed to find a navy blue full length dress for Nell which had little lace sleeves on the shoulders which looked like scallop shells. It would complement my dress beautifully. I was really pleased that we had sorted out the two dresses and as an extra, that my mam had also come across a beautiful dress in Binns which was a light green colour which really brought out the blue in her eyes. I couldn't wait to get back to see Red and tell him what a great day it had been and I knew that Red and I were also going to pop down to The Beach Grotto before evening to sort out some final bits of pieces for the food and drinks. It really was coming together so wonderfully and it was so exciting.

Red and I had also been trying to look at buying our first home together. We had looked at four houses but none of them seemed quite right for us. We looked at one in Harton and one in South Shields but I wanted to be nearer my parents as I knew Red would be working away soon. I really wanted to live in the village but houses were unfortunately only available to miners and their families so we had made the decision to look in nearby Whitburn. We had looked at the further two, one of which was too big and the other one needed a lot of fixing and I was getting really worried we were never going to find a house before Red had to go away. The fifth house we were going to look at had just come onto the market and was called 'Honeysuckle Cottage'. I loved the name of it and as we got to the street and glanced down to the house at the end, I grabbed Red's hand.

The little cottage at the end of the street was simply enchanting. Multi-coloured roses lined the little yellow path which wound from its wooden gate to the front door, their flowers gently bobbing in the summer breeze. The cottage itself was a pale yellow in colour and was covered in old wooden trellises which were entangled with golden-coloured honeysuckle flowers. Above the front of the door was a plaque which said, 'Honeysuckle Cottage' with tiny intricate yellow flowers in each corner and a boat underneath it. I nudged Red, it was a sign.

An elderly lady opened the door and greeted us and proceeded to show us around the cottage. The old lady explained that she had lived there for over sixty years with her husband who had regrettably passed away recently and she was in the process of moving to Newcastle to be nearer to her daughter. I noticed how the old lady looked sad as she told us this. The old lady showed us into the two cosy bedrooms upstairs and the little bathroom which was done out in a deep blue and crisp white, just like a sailor's uniform. The downstairs had a living room, a pantry and dining area and a large kitchen; to us it felt like a palace. I beamed at Red and the old lady smiled as she watched the two of us holding hands. The old lady led us out the back kitchen door and into the cottage's garden, it was beautiful. Either side of the grass were two beds awash with colour which drew your eye to the centre of the garden and focal point of the view: the North Sea as far as the eye could see. We could even hear the sound of the distant sea lapping against the cliffs. I squeezed Red's hand, he knew as well as I did that it would be perfect for us and I couldn't believe we were able to afford it. Red told the lady that we were very interested in the cottage and her wrinkled face smiled back at us. Later that day Red took care of business and formally put an offer in on Honeysuckle Cottage.

Red and I were so nervous for the next few days and we lived on tenterhooks. Four days after we had put the offer in on Honeysuckle Cottage, Red arrived unannounced at my parents' house.

"Lily," Red shouted up the stairs. I hurriedly made my way down the stairs as Red caught me at the bottom and lifted me up in the air, wildly spinning me round and then kissing me.

"Lil," Red smiled. "The offer was accepted, Honeysuckle Cottage is ours."

I was overjoyed. I couldn't believe that beautiful cottage would be ours. Red explained that the estate agent selling the cottage had received quite a lot of interest but we were the first couple to put an offer in on it. The old lady selling the house accepted our offer straight away and was apparently delighted to sell to a young couple who she felt would love the house as much as she did. As the old lady had already moved the majority of her things out, the sale of the house was likely to be very quick and it was possible that we could get the keys in a mere week, once we had sorted out the paperwork. I was speechless; here we were, Red and I, and in the next three weeks we would own a house together and be married. I held Red tightly and never wanted to let him go.

It was the week before the wedding when we were able to get the keys to 'Honeysuckle', as we now called it. Red collected me from my parents with the old brass key and we made the short ten-minute walk down to Whitburn and to Honeysuckle.

In the bright daylight, the cottage looked even more entrancing than we remembered. As we opened the little wooden gate, we made our way down the quaint paved path with each flower bobbing its head in turn for their new keepers and up to the front door. We carefully placed the key into the door and turned the lock. The front door creaked open allowing sunlight to slowly illuminate the room. We stepped in and took a moment to take in that this was our house now. I hugged Red and then we kissed lovingly. We walked around each room which was now empty apart from the sunlight, as we got to the kitchen we saw a little white envelope on the windowsill. Red took the envelope and I opened it, it was a little card with a picture of a boat on the front, I read it aloud.

'Dear Thom and Lily,
Congratulations on buying Honeysuckle Cottage and on your upcoming
marriage, I hope you have as many happy years in it as I did with my
husband. Please fill the house with love and laughter.

My dearest wishes,
Mrs Amelia Wren.

I was very touched by the old lady's kind words, it must have been very difficult for her to leave her home but at the same time she seemed genuinely pleased that we had bought it and I knew that we would honour her wishes.

We were eager to show Harry and Nell the cottage and we invited them to come to have a look around the following day. Red met me, Harry and Nell in the village and we made our way over to the cottage. I was giddy to show them it, my two oldest friends. I hoped they would love it as much as we did. When we got to the cottage door, Harry and Nell looked excited, we opened the door and they looked around, then they both came up and hugged me and Red.

"We are so proud of you both," said Nell to me and Red. "This is just perfect for you both and I am so glad you are still going to be so near us."

We all enjoyed a cup of tea that day in the back garden using some of our moving boxes as a table and a little bottle of milk which I had brought in my bag.

As the week progressed in the run up to the wedding, Nell was a great help to me and Harry was to Red. Nell helped organise the last bits and pieces for decorating The Beach Grotto and church and helped my mam and I sort out the wedding flowers. In the meantime, Harry and Red had moved some old furniture into Honeysuckle, cleaned and also unpacked some of mine and Red's belongings.

It was two days before the wedding and I could not believe the change in the cottage in just a few days. It was rapidly starting to feel like a home. Later on, Red and I were alone in the cottage unpacking further boxes when he took my hand and led me upstairs to what would become our bedroom. He nervously opened the door and there was a brand-new brass bed with rose pink-coloured sheets and pillows, a side dresser, some grey curtains, and a brand new grey rug.

"Do you like it, Lil?" Red queried.

I blushed and responded shyly, "I do, Red. It is lovely."

I knew we would be spending our wedding night in Honeysuckle. Red had been so thoughtful in making sure that our bedroom would be clean and ready for our first night as husband and wife. We went and lay on the bed together and kissed holding each other tightly.

"I love you, Lil," said Red.

"I love you too," I replied.

It would have been very easy to just stay there and give myself to Red but it would be even more special on our wedding night. It was something that I had been thinking about a lot recently. I was very excited to be with Red but also very nervous. What if I did something wrong? Red and I left the cottage and headed back to the village to meet Nell and Harry. We were going to The Beach Grotto that night for the final time as just me, Red, Nell and Harry. The next time Red and I would be Mr and Mrs Ayre. The Beach Grotto was in full swing and we all danced together and celebrated. I wasn't going to see Red on the day before the wedding so I made sure I gave him an extra big kiss that night.

The day before the wedding had arrived, my mam, Nell and I went to collect our dresses and to drop the flowers off at the church and The Beach Grotto. I knew Red was busy collecting suits and that Harry was helping him and then on the evening they were going to check everything was set up in the church and The Beach Grotto. That evening Nell was going to stay with me at my parents' so that we could get ready for the wedding together. We ate our home-cooked dinner with my mam and dad, my last dinner as Lily Smith in the house I had lived in for nineteen years. Part of me felt very sad that I was no longer an integral part of this little terrace's heartbeat but at the same time I could not wait for my new life with Red.

Nell and I went to my bedroom to go to bed, giggling as we climbed into the bed.

"Lil," said Nell, "I still can't believe it is yours and Red's wedding day tomorrow." She took my hand and gave it a kiss. "How are you feeling now?"

I felt ready. I wanted to marry Red and I wanted to become his wife and to share a life with him.

Nell chuckled and said somewhat cheekily, "And what about the night?"

I blushed. "Nell!" I exclaimed and laughed. "You don't ask ladies things like that! All I will say on the subject however, is that I am ready to become a woman," as the two of us collapsed into fits of laughter.

As we turned the light off and I could hear Nell breathing gently as she lay asleep beside me, I thought about the future and how my life would change. I would no longer live with my parents and didn't know what it would be like living with Red. I also knew I would have to be an adult and I would have responsibilities. Part of me was truly terrified at this prospect. I then thought of the day which lay ahead and of Red, his handsome face, his wonderful smile, muscular body, perfect mouth and his woody smell and I could not wait to give myself to him entirely.

LILY

25th May 1946

I woke with a startle. Nell was pulling the covers off me shouting "Come on." She was so excited and so was I. We went downstairs to have some light breakfast with my mam and dad who were also smiling from ear to ear. I could not believe that today was my wedding day, the joyous day when Red and I would become man and wife and we would belong to one another.

We still had lots of things to do this morning and I knew Red and Harry were doing the final finishes to the church and The Beach Grotto. My dad excused himself as he had to go and help Red and Harry. Nell and I sat at the old wooden table as my mam, wearing her trusty pinny, hummed to herself as she started to do mine and Nell's hair. My mam carefully heated the old curling tongs and slid them delicately through Nell's hair first, pinning up the white blonde ringlets as she went. She then moved onto my chestnut locks and curled them round the tongs spraying lacquer as she went. The next thing she did was put her hand in her pocket and pulled out an ornate-looking hair slide. It was silver with mother of pearl tiny flowers surrounding its edge; it was beautiful and I had never seen it before.

My mam placed the slide in my hair and pinned and lacquered it in place and then explained in a quiet voice, "This was my grandmother's, Lily. It can be your something borrowed and your something old."

I beamed at my mam. It was very special, just like her.

After our hair was finished, Nell and I went upstairs to do each other's make-up. I was only getting married once so decided I wanted to look like a film star from one of the Hollywood movies, which gave me so much joy. Nell had bought some new make-up for the day and she carefully lined my eyes with a kohl pencil and flicked them on the edges. She then put lashings of mascara on and covered my face in a peach-coloured powder.

"Wow, Lily," gasped Nell, "you do look like a star." She then did her make-up in a similar way to match. We heard my dad coming back through the door downstairs.

"The church must be ready," I whispered to Nell and squeezed her hands with delight.

We started to get our dresses on. I helped Nell with hers first as she pulled up her navy blue dress with her little lace-capped sleeves which perfectly set off her white blonde hair. I stepped into my dress next and delicately placed my arms through the intricate lace sleeves, as Nell gently pulled up the bodice and did up one tiny button after the other until she reached the uppermost one. Nell then went and pulled a carefully wrapped item from her bag; it was the veil she had made for me. I daintily pulled the tissue paper apart and underneath was a skilful blend of lace and chiffon. I wanted to cry as I slowly lifted the veil out of the paper to reveal its full splendour.

"Nell, this is beautiful," I said as I felt a small tear come to my eye.

Nell calmly placed the veil on my head, its full length reaching past the bottom of my dress with the lace edging swathing my bedroom floor. I never dreamt Nell would make something like this and it was perfect. Nell wiped my tear away.

"Don't cry, Lil, you will set me off and besides, I have already done your make-up," Nell laughed. "It is your something new from me."

I hugged Nell close and said, "And you, my darling girl, are my something blue."

We looked at each other in the mirror and I savoured our reflection which showed a very special bond with a lifelong friend.

Nell then reached for her bag. "Wait," she said, as she pulled out two new lipsticks. She placed the pale pink one onto her lips and then put my colour on my lips, it was a bright vivid red. Nell shrugged and laughed. "What other colour would it have been? You look beautiful, now let's get you downstairs."

As I took those final steps down the staircase I had known all my life, I felt nervous going in to see my mam and dad. My mam had already seen the dress so I knew she liked it but what would my dad think? I cautiously entered the cosy little living room for the last time as Miss Smith. My dad looked up transfixed, he then beamed with pride and his hazel eyes glistened as he held my mam's hand.

"Lily, my beautiful daughter," my Dad said as he then handed me my white roses as Nell picked up her smaller posy. We were all ready now, my olive-coloured dad resplendent in a navy suit and my golden blonde mam looking lovely in her light green dress. They really were a striking couple.

I took a deep breath as we left the terrace, my terrace, and my home up until this point. Things would never be the same again but I was ready to make this change. My dad offered his strong protective arm and linked in with mine to make the short walk to the church whilst my mam and Nell linked arms. It was only a five-minute walk but it felt like an eternity, I could not wait to see my Red again. As we entered the church yard my mam kissed me on the cheek and then kissed my dad as she went to enter to take her seat.

Nell carefully arranged my dress and placed my veil neatly as we took our steps towards the church door. I leaned on my dad slightly and took a deep breath as I entered the door to the sound of the antique organ playing the opening bars of the wedding march and I took in the musky smell of the church. I had only one focus now, Red.

I could see him at the altar, resplendent in his navy suit. He looked so smart, his russet hair shining from the sunlit streaks that poured through the jewel-coloured church windows. My dad and I walked past the lines of the timeworn mahogany pews filled with the comforting smiling faces of the village, including Harry and Nell's parents, who had come to celebrate our marriage with us. The pure white roses at the altar glimmered as we made our way towards them, Harry watched us all with pride and looked incredibly smart as we neared him and Red. The walk seemed to last forever until we ultimately got to the altar. I was finally side by side with Red; he turned to look at me and his whole face radiated with delight as he revealed one of his wonderful smiles. My dad gave my hand to Red's on instruction by the vicar and the wedding ceremony began. I was giddy with life at this point and can only properly remember certain parts of the ceremony. We did our first hymn together – 'Lord of all Hopefulness', one of my favourites – and Nell did a reading for us from the Bible. The vicar then took charge again and asked Harry for the rings which we had picked together and which were plain silver bands. As the vicar placed the rings on the Bible the light caught them and they sparkled at us.

Red and I took each other's hands, I remember hearing, "Do you, Lillian Margaret Smith, take Thom Ayre to be your lawfully wedded husband?" to which I responded gleefully, "I do" and then we said our vows to each other out loud which was all a bit of a blur. I looked down at my hand at the endless silver band which Red had lovingly placed on my finger as the vicar announced that we were now husband and wife and that Red may now kiss the bride. As Red leaned in to kiss me, it was like an electric charge going through my body. I kissed him back and held his hand tightly. I had missed him so much and we had only been apart two days.

We did our final hymn in the church which was 'Eternal Father', an ode to Red's time as a sailor and also to our love of the sea. Red took my hand as the organ began to play 'All Things Bright and Beautiful' as we left the little church together hand in hand as husband and wife.

We made the short walk to the Rattler which was gleaming in the sunlight and covered in pastel-coloured bunting. Mr Gunn got the Rattler engine ready as Harry helped his dad to get the wedding guests into its little carriages. The village, my family, my Nell and Harry and my Red all travelled along the beautiful coast to The Beach Grotto in the rackety carriages as one of the members of the miners' band played the trumpet. I leant my head on Red's shoulder and I could not have wished for anything more.

At The Beach Grotto, Red and I took the first lift down to our reception room as the rest of the guests either waited for the next lift or took the white steps down to the beach. Red and I knew we had a few minutes to ourselves as the lift scaled the side of the cliff down to the beach. Red gave me that wonderful smile as he placed his arms around my waist and leaned in and whispered, "I love you, Lily, my beautiful wife. I am such a lucky man."

I grabbed the back of his head and pulled him in towards me as we kissed passionately – our first as husband and wife. The bell in the lift rang as we approached the beach and we laughed as we pulled apart from each other and I wiped lipstick off his lips and we straightened ourselves out.

As the lift doors opened, The Beach Grotto looked truly enchanting. The main area had been set up formally with tables stretching over half the space with an area for the miners' band and dance floor for the evening celebrations. Despite it being a sunny day, the oil lamps in The Beach Grotto were lit illuminating the little hollows with their firefly like glow. The tables were covered with white linen and had large silver candlesticks in the middle which were surrounded by white roses. The doors which led to the patio were open and the patio area had been cleared into an open space so that this could also be used for the evening celebrations. Red and Harry had done such a good job in helping get everything set up and I was incredibly thankful to them. The guests were starting to mill around in the patio area now and were helping themselves to the perry which we offered. Red and I also took a glass as we mingled with our guests. We could see Harry and Nell making their way up the steps to the patio from the beach; Nell ran towards me and we hugged and then Harry joined in too.

"We are so unbelievably happy for you, Lil," said Nell as she then bent to dutifully straighten my dress.

Harry took my hand and kissed it. "Lily, you look just perfect, I am so proud of you," said Harry.

Red came over and hugged us all too as it was announced we were to take our seats for dinner.

We all tucked into the food as it was served, the pale pink prawns in their crisp lettuce bed and then a roast beef dinner with Yorkshire pudding and spring vegetables washed down by a choice of either red or white wine. It was deliciously decadent. As I looked around the room I was warmed by all our guests smiling and laughing happily and I was so pleased that Red and I could share this moment with them.

The speeches then followed, I knew my dad, Red and Harry would be nervous for them and that they would not fully relax until they were finished. My dad, who did not like public speaking, took a gulp of his wine and then he stood up, his hazel eyes filling as he began to speak in a clear voice:

"To our friends and family on this special day which means so much to me, I want to thank you all first for coming and I hope you are enjoying the day so far. I would like to thank Nell and Harry, who both look wonderful today, for all their help and support on the planning of the wedding. I also want to welcome Red formally to our family, a man with a heart of gold. We couldn't wish for a better husband for our daughter Lillian. Maggie and I feel like we have gained a new son rather than lost a daughter. That brings me on to my beloved wife, Maggie. Thank you for helping me raise this beautiful woman that I have the honour of calling my daughter and who I am so proud of today. Lily, our daughter, you brought light into mine and your mam's life; a true gift from above. We have loved raising you and watching you grow from that little dark-haired baby, to a little independent girl, to the young woman you have become today, not only beautiful but also clever. Your mam and I wish you every success in your future. To the new Mr and Mrs Ayre we wish you a lifetime of laughter together and a strong and happy marriage. Please could you all raise your glasses to Lily and Red."

Everybody applauded as my dad bowed to take his seat again. I squeezed my dad's hand as he sat down; it was a lovely speech and I knew he would have felt uncomfortable doing it.

Next was Red. As my handsome husband lifted himself out of his chair I thought how lucky I was that I could call this charming man mine, I felt very blessed. Red cleared his throat and began to speak:

"I would like to start by thanking everyone for coming today and to Mike and Maggie for their kind hospitality in hosting the wedding. I have felt so welcomed into their family and it has been an honour to become part of it formally today. To Nell, you look beautiful today and I want to thank you personally for everything you have done to help Lily and support her with the wedding and with helping us buy our house together. Also to Harry for agreeing to be my best man and for allowing me, an outsider, to join the famous Marsden trio, I look forward to many happy years together with you both. Lastly to my wife, Lily, who today is the most exquisite woman I have ever seen in my life, I am privileged to just be allowed to stand here next to you, never mind call you my wife. From the moment we met, there was a vibrancy in you which I had never come across before, your strong love for your family and friends and your kindness with children. I was honoured when you accepted my wedding proposal and I look forward to starting this new chapter of our lives together. I am proud to stand here in front of everyone and say how much I love you. Please, could we all raise a toast to my beautiful, clever, funny, and wonderful wife, Lily."

I felt my face flush as Red sat back down amongst applause. I was flattered by his words and that he had spoken about me like that in front of everyone. I couldn't wait to get him on his own. I smiled at him in complete admiration and he smiled back.

Harry was next to do his best man's speech, he stood up and winked at me and started:

"It is a true honour to be here today at Red and Lily's wedding and to be able to be best man for this wonderful pair. Firstly, thank you again to Maggie and Mike for hosting this beautiful day. Next, as the best man, I would like to personally thank the bridesmaid, Nell, for all her help with the wedding and who looks wonderful today, her partner is a lucky fella. Hey, Nell, you know what everyone says about best men and bridesmaids."

The guests all laughed, Nell went crimson and Red and I chuckled. Harry continued:

"To Red, thank you for letting me be your best man, it is such an honour for me to be part of Lily and yours wedding but I was thrilled to be able to be the best man. Red, we have become really close in the past few months and you will be the perfect match for Lily. Finally, to Lily, my beautiful, dearest friend, having met when we were just tiny, I can't imagine my life without you in it. From playing on the beach, games in the lighthouse, and going to school together, you are a sister to me and I am so pleased that you are happy and that you married the love of your life today, you also look absolutely flawless. Today we celebrate the marriage of Lily and Red, my two best friends coming together as one. I hope your marriage shines as brightly as our lighthouse. To Lily and Red."

I was very touched by Harry's words, he really was a huge part of my life too and I couldn't imagine if either he or Nell were not a part of it.

After the speeches, Red and I cut our wedding cake which had been made by Red's mam, who was a talented baker. The wedding guests moved out onto the patio area which was basked in beautiful sunshine as the cake was distributed and sparkling perry was given out whilst Red and I went for some wedding photos.

The first photo was in front of the commanding presence of Marsden Rock and its seabirds with Harry and Nell by our sides, the four of us giggled as the gentle breeze caught mine and Nell's dresses and gently blew our hair. Harry and Nell went back to The Beach Grotto after that and Red and I got some further photos standing on the beach with the vast sea as the backdrop and then some very personal ones for us of us in front of the cliffs and our cave.

I turned to Red and kissed him. "It has been such a wonderful day," I declared.

"It's not over yet, Lil, we still have the evening to go," Red said happily.

"Oh no, our dance," I exclaimed to Red.

I remembered in the haste of buying the house and planning the wedding that we had not picked a song for our first dance.

Red placed his finger against my lips and smoothly said, "Don't worry, Lil. I picked one."

I wasn't sure what he had picked but I was quite pleased he had at least thought of one. We made our way back to The Beach Grotto and our guests. As the weather was exceptionally mild and still sunny the miners' band moved themselves out onto the patio and set themselves up there; they also brought out a microphone. The guests were getting ready for the party, drinks were flowing and Red and I managed to get around to speak everyone. The next thing the miners' band had taken their places and Harry was at the microphone.

"'Red, Lily, can you come onto this dance floor please?'" boomed Harry's voice through the speaker.

Red and I stood in the middle of floor and I was intrigued to find out the song that Red had chosen for us to have our first dance to as husband and wife.

Harry then began to speak again. "My dearest Lily and Red, I present a gift to you both from myself, Nell and the band."

Nell, who was standing near to Harry, then took over and Harry joined the band, as the brass played the opening bars Red spun me around and I knew it was 'My Romance', the song which played on the night we met. Nell's velvety smooth tones drifted the length of the beach as Red took me in his arms and held me close. I was so moved by the day, the emotion of the song, my handsome and thoughtful Red and the effort that Nell, Harry and the band must have had to go into to learn the song, that a single tear fell down my cheek. Red held me tightly as we rocked from side to side with the music. As Nell's smooth tones were nearing the end of the song Red opened my arms up and spun me around so that the white skirt of my dress spun as it caught the breeze. The band then struck up again and they played some great party music; the brass really changed the mood to a party atmosphere and everyone danced in glee. At nine p.m. we had arranged for the landlord to play the latest hits so that the band and Nell and Harry could really join in. I danced with Nell, then Harry and then we all danced in a circle, it was raucous fun.

Red had arranged for a taxi to collect us at eleven p.m. to take us to our new home, although it was not a far walk from The Beach Grotto, I was pleased I did not have to walk it in my wedding dress. We said our goodbyes to the guests, to Nell and Harry and to our families as we made our way to the lift. We repeated where we had left in the lift and kissed each other passionately until we got to the top and into the taxi which was waiting for us. We held hands for the short distance until we pulled up to our charming Honeysuckle, our first home together. Red led me up to the front door as he then told me to wait, quickly ran into the cottage and I could hear him going up the stairs. When he got back to the front door, he lifted me over the entrance as I giggled. We locked the door and then

Red led me up the stairs to our bedroom. Inside the bedroom, Red had lit several candles and a small lamp, there was a change of clothes for both of us laying on the side dresser as well as a few toiletries. He really had thought of everything. Red went to close the curtains and there was a new plant on the old windowsill, it was a vibrant red lily and on one side was a chilled bottle of wine and the other, two glasses.

Red laughed and said, "What do you think of my new plant? I thought it was appropriate?"

I moved towards Red and took his hand. "I couldn't think of anything more perfect," I said.

I felt nervous now but ready.

Red took my other hand and whispered, "Lil, you really took my breath away today, I love you so much my stunning wife."

I replied by telling him how much I loved him too. I turned my back to him as he caressed my neck and slowly undid each intricate button and peeled the sleeves down my arms until my wedding dress fell to the floor.

I turned to face him as he looked at my figure. "You are so beautiful," Red said as he kissed my mouth as we moved onto the bed.

Red took his shirt off and I felt his skin touch mine; he lovingly explored every inch of my body, I had never felt anything like it before. He then moved his muscular frame on top of mine as we tenderly gave ourselves to each other.

We were husband and wife now and it was the most natural end to the most special day of my life.

ANNA

April 2017

The image of my gran's upset face remained embedded in my mind, something which I could not allow to become a reality. James and I had made the final decision that we would get married in the North East, it was our heritage and a part of us and I couldn't bear to not have all my family at our wedding. I had talked it through with James and I also decided that I still wanted Nora to be my bridesmaid, even though she had chosen not to have me as her bridesmaid and she had deeply upset me recently. She was still my oldest friend.

James and I had spent a few long weeks looking at several wedding venues in the North East but we still hadn't found one which was quite right for us. We would continue to look but we had Nora and Tim's hen and stag parties to look forward to at the weekend. Despite Nora's recent behaviour, I was looking forward to her hen party as it had been a busy few weeks at work and Sarah, Tim's sister, and Nora's bridesmaid, had planned to have a girly weekend away in Marbella, whereas the stag was at a golf resort in Portugal. Both flights to Marbella and Portugal were from London airport so James and I had decided to take a week off either side of the hen and stag celebrations and have a night either side in London too. I was looking forward to the break away in the sunshine with my friends and to escape and spend some quality time with James away from wedding planning and work.

There had been a bit of a divide amongst the girls' group in relation to Nora's hen. Sarah's choice of Marbella had irked a few of the other girls due to the cost and the holiday that needed to be taken from work to attend. Sarah's initial budgeting of £650 each for the weekend had been met with contempt from some of the girls and I must admit, I thought it was a lot for a weekend away and wondered what on earth we would be doing. I had encouraged Sarah to try and get the cost below at least £500 per person to try and allow more people to attend, which she had managed with a lot of moaning by booking rooms in a less exclusive villa, I started to wonder just what kind of world Tim and Sarah had come from where money, it seemed, grew on trees.

On our day off, James and I made our way down to London by train, a journey which I always enjoyed. We had booked to go first class, as again related to food, we both really enjoyed getting our lunch served in the pleasant surroundings of the cosy carriage. There was something rather decadent about eating newly baked cakes, rustic sandwiches, hand-cooked crisps and freshly brewed tea as the English countryside whooshed by. As the train had just departed York, I received a phone call from my boss so I went to stand in the train vestibule.

"Anna, how are you and apologies for calling on your day off."

I told her that was okay.

"I know that you are off until Tuesday and that you are in London until then but Al wants to have a meeting with you in the London office on Tuesday. It's nothing to worry about and, in fact, an opportunity but I can't say anything more about it just yet. Would you be able to meet him say about ten a.m. and of course, you don't need to take the day as holiday anymore as it is such short notice?"

I thought for a moment as the train back was at one p.m. so it would give me time to meet Al who was the managing partner of the firm.

"Yes, I can do that," I said.

"That is great news, Anna. Al will be delighted," my boss responded. "I will let him know."

I hurried back to my chair where James was sat with a curious expression.

"Well," remarked James, "What was that about?"

I explained to James how I was going to meet Al on Tuesday and how the opportunity intrigued me. I nuzzled into James and said, "Anyhow, I am going to try not to think about it. I want to enjoy the time with you tonight and then the Marbella weekend."

That evening in London with James, just me and him, was just wonderful. We saw a show, had a fantastic meal and spent some wonderful time together. As I lay in the sumptuous hotel bed with James quietly snoozing beside me, I did wonder what the meeting with Al was going to be like and imagined the various scenarios that it could be. I am glad my boss had said it was nothing to worry about as otherwise I would have spent wasted time worrying and imagining the worst possible situations. I sighed, released my thoughts and looked at James's gorgeous face as I lay my arm over him and dozed off ready for the weekend ahead.

James and I made our way together to Gatwick Airport to get our respective flights for the weekend. As we reached the departure lounge we could see a gaggle of girls with brightly-coloured feathers and sashes and in the middle was somebody wearing pure white. James raised his eyebrows at me as it then became clear that this was the hen party. As we approached the group, the pure white figure was Nora. I gasped at her appearance as she was a shadow of her former self and couldn't help feeling very sad for her, even though she appeared to be happy. The white silk slip-like dress she was wearing was very beautiful but it clung to her now painfully thin body. Her hair was done in a beehive style and piled on her head with tendrils framing her once full face which had now been replaced by hollowed out eyes, sunken cheek bones and a jutting collarbone. Nora had obviously taken the dieting too far and I hoped that once the wedding was over, she would regain her former glorious figure.

"Anna, James," Nora shrilled as she mooched over to hug us. "James, Tim is over there," she said as she pointed to the bar.

James kissed me and said his goodbyes as he headed off to the stag as I was promptly handed a sash and some pink feathers to wear by Sarah the bridesmaid. Jo, Kate and Zoe were all attending the hen too, so I went to stand with them whilst we waited for the flight. The flight itself was fine and Sarah had bought everyone prosecco to get everyone in the party mood, which was kind of her. As we made our way to the arrivals in Marbella airport, the heat washed over us as the glorious sun shone brightly. As we stepped outside we were blinded by a silver flash of light which once our eyes adjusted, uncovered a huge white stretch limo. Nora shrieked with delight and all the girls looked excited as we clambered into the luxury compartment and made ourselves comfortable, but this time with chilled champagne. I was really starting to relax and looking forward to the weekend and it was lovely to see glimpses of the old Nora coming back. The limo pulled up to one of the most stunning villas I have ever seen in my life. Bright white walls which were nestled in the hills with views over the beach and with its own private pool, I couldn't believe we were going to spend the weekend here, it looked simply amazing. There were twelve girls in total and five large double bedrooms, one of which had two double beds, so the decision had been made that myself, Zoe, Jo and Kate would share the four-bed room as we all knew each other well, Nora was going to share with Sarah and the other girls would take the other rooms.

The hen party spent the afternoon in the villa and Sarah had arranged for a mobile chef to come and do a pool BBQ. As all the girls lay around the poolside with the smell of chargrilled fresh meat and seafood filling the air and the prosecco flowing freely, everyone looked to be having a lovely time.

Kate sipped her prosecco and said, "I still can't believe this place Nora, it is incredible."

At this point Sarah smirked. "You should have seen the other place I wanted to book, it was much nicer. It's the villa we stayed in before Nora."

Nora, who had on a new designer bikini which unfortunately again showed off just how thin and fragile looking she had become, stomped her foot and remarked, "I loved it there; we should have gone there instead!"

Kate looked embarrassed. I am not sure if Nora had completely forgotten a world where money was not an issue or if she was just a bit drunk and emotional, but I quickly tried to change the subject.

"Who wants a dip in the pool?" I yelled as I jumped into the deep end of the pool and tried to encourage others to join me.

As we all dried off after being in the pool, we enjoyed eating the array of barbequed delights that were lain out in front of us. Even Nora tucked into her small plate of prawns with gusto as she let her guard down. Sarah had arranged for the limo to take us all into the town that evening for a cocktail making class in one of the 'trendiest' nightclubs that Marbella had to offer. For the hour before the limo picked us up we all became young girls again, doing each other's hair and makeup and getting ready in our dresses for the night that lay ahead. Everyone was excited for the cocktail class. As the limo pulled up to our villa, all the ladies looked exceptional and we climbed in one by one as we made our way to Playa, which was apparently the hottest club in Marbella. The limo made the short journey down the mountainside and pulled up in front of a white fortress-looking building, its neon lights penetrating the cobbled street in front of it and heat eliminating from the large fiery sculptures that encased its entrance. Two topless waiters made their way down to the limo, one holding the door open and winking as we stepped out one by one and the other holding a tray of mojitos, as the first one led us into the club and to a cordoned off area within the VIP section. Carlos, the first waiter, as we came to know, was to be our instructor for the evening. We all watched intently as he threw the colourful bottles around his body and manoeuvred dry ice into waspish creations. All the cocktails he made were exceptional and Nora squealed with delight when he made a signature cocktail, The Nora, for her with her favourite ingredients of cassis, prosecco, and lime. The whole group of girls knocked back a few of the Nora's as we took to the dance floor in the VIP area and danced together.

The music was blasting out of the huge sound system and our gang of girls was starting to get infiltrated by men. How I did not miss this aspect of going to clubs, as a tanned male's hand appeared on my shoulder. I swiftly brushed it off and made my exit from the dance floor to go and sit at the bar. Carlos was still behind the private bar, so I went and sat at the bar with him and ordered another drink. Carlos was a nice chap and was studying to become a lawyer at the local university whilst working at the club for some extra money, so I chatted and joked with him behind the bar.

I soon felt a pair of eyes staring at me. It was Nora, who was now very drunk, as she then proceeded to march over and yell at me, "You just have to have all the attention, don't you!"

I was quite taken aback. Kate and Jo tried to calm a hysterical Nora down as we attempted to gather up all the girls and get them back into the limo.

At the villa, we got Nora into bed and I sat with Kate outside. "I don't know what that was about," I explained to Kate. "I was on the dance floor and then this bloke kept putting his hand on me, so I went to sit at the bar. I was only chatting to Carlos about his studies; he's training to become a lawyer."

From what Kate could piece together by Nora's yelling and crying to Sarah, Carlos had not winked at her when she had gotten out the limo and she had taken this personally that as the bride, all attention should be on her, similarly with on the dance floor.

"That is ridiculous," I said, "She was wearing a sash with 'bride' written on it so obviously men are not going to fall at her feet!"

I lay awake in bed that night and could not understand Nora's logic or her problem. I really did not miss nights out like those or nights out as a single woman and just longed to be in James's arms. I also kept thinking how yes, that was a nice nightclub but it was no better than any other in Newcastle. I thought about how the stag was going and I texted James goodnight as I wondered what the next day would bring.

Sunlight flooded the white walls of the villa as the girls all made a sluggish entrance into the pool area for brunch.

Nora came in and smiled at me, obviously oblivious to how she had behaved the night before. I decided to just leave it and not talk to her about last night as I didn't want to cause more tension on her hen party. Sarah had organised for everyone to go on a four-hour catamaran tour for the afternoon's activities. I was quite looking forward to this although I wasn't sure how everyone's stomachs would fare! The private chef in the villa was a godsend; he rustled up freshly squeezed orange juice, pastries and pancakes which seemed to help the pounding heads of a few of the girls. As we left the villa to make the journey to the port we could see the vast catamaran sitting in the glistening water. This trip was just what everyone needed.

The salty sea air, glass bottom of the catamaran which uncovered the hidden depths of the sea and luxurious deck loungers, eased the whole group's tension and allowed everyone to relax. As the catamaran soared in and out of various inlets of water, we got to see a hidden side of Marbella and got to swim in calm and tranquil waters away from the bustle of the town, I couldn't help but think of home and how it reminded me of the coastline there, albeit with a slightly different temperate.

I thought of my gran and what she would make of this hen party and the affluence of it all and the change in Nora's behaviours. I knew my gran would tell me to be loyal to Nora but I still couldn't help but feel hurt by her actions. I understood why she might want her new sister-in-law to be her bridesmaid but it still hurt me not to have been asked and not to have been involved in any of the planning of the hen party. I couldn't help but feel that this extravagant holiday was more about Sarah showing off how much money the family had, rather than it being a personal celebration for Nora and her marriage, still there had been no mention of Tim. I sighed as I spread my body out across the lounger as I let the warm sun relax my body. I made a mental note to ask my gran if she'd had a hen party when I got back home.

Sunday was the last full day in the villa before the hens and stags travelled back home. I thought that Sarah might have organised something special for the final day but instead the itinerary from eleven a.m. to five p.m. was stated as FREE TIME. I found this a little odd and I know some of the other girls did too; why get us all out to Spain then not have something planned? As it got to ten a.m. it suddenly became very clear that Sarah had organised something, just not for us. Sarah was taking Nora out on a private yacht for lunch and to sunbathe. I did think this was a nice thing for Sarah to do for Nora, just perhaps not when we were all still in Marbella. Sarah had made a sarcastic comment to the group about 'people not wanting to pay' for the yacht so she had just organised it herself. As Sarah and Nora left in their finery to go and board the yacht, the remaining ten of us sat in the villa like spare parts.

We lay about the pool for an hour or so in the heat and then I turned to Kate and said, "This is ridiculous, we are sitting about here just doing nothing when we could be doing something. I am going to walk down to the old town, do you fancy coming?"

Kate nodded and as our plans trickled through to the rest of the group all ten of us then got changed, put on our flat shoes and made the ten-minute walk down the dusty road to the old town. The buildings in this part of the town were old, sandy, flat roofed and beautiful. They looked like they had stories to tell and I much preferred them to the modern white duplexes. We absorbed the sights and sounds of the locals going about their Sunday chores speaking in their ornate fast spoken and passionate language. A smell of olive oil and chorizo led us down a small alley and to a worn building which had a sign outside saying 'Tapas'.

The girls all read the sign and smiled at each other hungrily and we marched in happily. The view from this small restaurant was incredible and overlooked the bay of Marbella. The owner came to the table and recommended we try the tapas and he said he would just bring a selection along with jugs of sangria. We all grinned back at him like Cheshire cats. As the sea breeze wafted through the open windows we drank the fresh and invigorating sangria as dish upon dish of colourful jewels were brought to our wooden table. We heartily tucked in to bowls of spicy chorizo in red wine, vine tomatoes drizzled in balsamic, prawns in garlic and lemon on little wooden sticks, herby meatballs the size of a fist, saffron paella with chicken, ham croquettes in a cheesy sauce and freshly baked crusty bread to mop up all the sauces. At the end the whole group was stuffed. It was such a wonderful meal with lovely company, we all laughed as the sangria flowed but I couldn't help but feel upset for Nora that she had missed out, well the old Nora that is, she would have loved this enjoying nice food with friends where the focus is on the food not the location. The owner charged us 30 Euro per head for all the food and sangria, it was amazing. We all left 35 Euro each as we had enjoyed it so much. We slowly made our way back up to the villa and we all lay by the poolside and had a little siesta as we waited for our bride and the host to return from their yacht outing.

Nora and Sarah returned just after six p.m. with Nora looking happy as she boasted about what she had done and seen on the yacht. It did sound very nice but I couldn't help but feel as if Nora perhaps enjoyed the recalling of the time on the yacht rather than the actual time itself. When Nora heard what we had all done for the day she sneered at the idea of eating in the old town and why we wanted to go there and not to the modern bay area, as her and Sarah laughed but as someone who had known her a very long time, I could recognise a split second of disappointment that she had not been included.

Sunday evening was a very quiet affair and was spent just in the villa with the chef doing a light supper for everyone in preparation for the early morning flight back to London. I was looking forward to going home; it had been a bit of a strange weekend.

After the five a.m. short flight back to the UK, I made my way by cab back to the London hotel where James and I were staying for the night until I had my meeting with Al the following day. I got the key to the hotel room and hastily went into the peaceful room, threw my bag on the hotel logo emblazoned carpet, shut the hefty curtains on the hustle and bustle of a Monday morning in busy London, stripped off my clothes and jumped into the crisp linen of the newly cleaned bed. As I stretched my body out against the sheets, I planned to have a few hours sleep before James was expected to arrive. I couldn't wait to see him. At what must have been midday I was awoken by the hotel door being pushed against the security chain.

"Anna," a voice called out. It was James.

I pushed my hair over my head and wrapped my body in the bed sheet as I went to let him in. We shut the door behind us as I went to hug James.

"I have missed you so much," I murmured as I held his body close to mine.

James dropped his bag and kissed my mouth as his hands moved down around the sheet. He moved back from me and raised an eyebrow as he peered down underneath the bed sheet.

"Anna," he exclaimed cheekily as he lifted me onto the bed and without saying a further word stripped off too and joined me under the bed sheet.

We reunited, as our bodies became one and we made love.

"Well, that was a lovely welcome," laughed James. I giggled as I held him close.

"I was only having a nap," I said. "I must have overslept, it's a nice way to spend an afternoon though," I said as we both laughed together.

"What was the stag like?" I asked.

"It was nice, Anna, I think Tim enjoyed it," James said. "But it wasn't really for me, there was a lot of golfing, sitting around and drinking port and talks of money," exclaimed James.

I had to laugh at the notion of my fiancé joining in these activities as he was perfectly happy with a pint, a pie and watching a footy match and although he worked very hard and earned his own successes, was certainly not one to talk about money.

James then asked about the hen party and what it was like.

"Similar." I laughed. "I think Nora enjoyed it but it was quite excessive and I think she could have had just as nice a time in the UK."

We both smiled and held each other as we decided at once that we would be having our hen and stag parties in Newcastle for ease and cost, as well as for our enjoyment. We were naughty for the rest of that day and we couldn't be bothered to leave the hotel room. James ordered up room service and a bottle of red and we devoured the lot in bed.

Tuesday came and I got myself ready to go and meet Al, not really knowing what to expect, whilst James sorted out the bags and the check out from the hotel. I took the murky Tube the three stops to the London office and was ushered into a meeting room by the receptionist.

Al bounded into the room to greet me.

"Anna, how lovely to see you and thank you so much for agreeing to meet me today, you must be wondering what this is all about?" I smiled and nodded at Al.

I had always liked him he was a very intelligent man and partner of a law firm but never lost his ability to speak to every single person he ever met as an equal.

"Yes," I said. "I am intrigued," as I smiled again.

"Well Anna," Al said. 'As you know, we are looking to expand the London office which has been doing really well and we are looking to branch out into commercial law from this office too. As you are now the most senior commercial lawyer in the North East office, I wanted to personally offer you the opportunity for an eighteen-month contract to head up and recruit a commercial team here in London."

I was gobsmacked, I certainly wasn't expecting this.

Al continued, "It would be a London salary and the firm would of course offer you accommodation whilst you are here. I know it is a big decision to make but I have been really impressed with your work ethic and ability over the years and wanted to offer you the post first before it was advertised. I certainly don't expect a decision today and will send you over all the finite detail of the role but I wanted to do the offer face-to-face."

I felt very proud that my work had been recognised but I didn't know what to do. I thanked Al for the opportunity and said I would need to go through the details. As I made my way to Kings Cross to meet my waiting James, I was still in shock. James had bought me a hot chocolate and I proceeded to tell him all about my job offer but it would mean being away from home during the week. James was ever the perfect fiancé and knew how big a career opportunity this could be for me and said he would support my decision whatever but that it had to be my decision.

As the train made its way up North, I quietly contemplated the job offer as James read his book. I was in quite a quandary; at least Al had allowed me some thinking time. I looked out the window at the rugged beauty of the North East coastline which embossed the midnight blue waters; as the train neared our destination, could I swap my life at this coast, my coast, for life in the big city? The train meandered alongside the river and into the heart of Newcastle, passing one old bridge after the other like loyal and faithful friends. Could I bring myself to leave my James during the week when I had missed him for just a weekend and could I bear to not see my family during the week and my precious gran?

I didn't know the answers but only time would tell.

LILY

June 1946

It was three weeks until Red was due to go to sea, a mere twenty-one days left with him until we were parted for nigh on six months and I was starting to get restless on an evening as I dreaded the distance that would come between us. Red and I didn't have a honeymoon, as Red had to go back to work immediately to complete the work on the ship to make sure it was ready for its voyage. On the days I didn't work I would go down to the shipyard to eat lunch with Red and to spend some precious time with him. We were newlyweds then and I remember one of those visits clearly.

It was a sunny Friday afternoon in June and I was wearing a dainty floral yellow sundress which flattered my feminine figure. The cargo ship was predominantly built with just a few bits left to do on the main deck and in the engine room. When I got to the shipyard the ship, 'Ruthy Ann' looked resplendent in the sunshine. Her 400ft long steel presence commanded your attention with her freshly painted funnel and intricate network of wooden masts and varnished floors. I felt very proud that Red had been part of the team who had produced such a feat of engineering and that Ruthy Ann was a South Shields lass, born and bred. I noticed how quiet it was, which was unusual. The foreman, Mr Frank, saw me as he was packing up his things.

"Hello Lily," he said. "How are you today? We ended up ahead of schedule this week, so I said everyone could finish a little earlier, given that we are going away in a few weeks. Red was finishing in the engine room and said he would lock the yard on his way out. Just go through."

I thanked him and carefully made my way with my little paper lunch bag up the rope lined shaky ramp and onto the ship's deck, the musky smell of oil mixed with fresh paint filled my lungs as I took careful paces down the shiny glossed wooden stairs to the engine room. When I reached the open door of the engine room I could already feel the heat coming out of it. I could hear a pummelling noise as I peered round the door and I could see Red. I took a deep breath. Red was working away with some kind of tool on a section of the engine, however what caught my attention was that he was wearing just a tight white vest and loose overall bottoms, his muscles glistening in the faint light of the engine room. His russet hair and body was streaked with oil. I stared at him like that for at least five minutes as my pulse began to race. Red could stir up feelings inside me which I had never experienced before; I don't know what came over me but I dropped the sandwich bag, I went up behind Red and put my arms around his waist.

"Lily," exclaimed Red as he put the tool down and turned around to face me.

I lifted his vest up over his head and pressed my mouth against his. He took me in his muscular arms and lifted me over to the engine room door and locked it behind us. He undid my sundress to expose my figure as he slid down his overalls. I wrapped my legs around his body as he lifted me up onto one of the benches clearing off the tools with his arm. I purred with pleasure as our bodies intertwined and we made love to each other without delay. Afterwards, we lay on the bench in each other's arms as we got our breath back, sweat dripping down our bodies. Red turned his face to mine.

"Well that was a pleasant surprise," he laughed as he raised one eyebrow up at me.

I blushed as I giggled back at him, and said coyly, "You just looked so handsome, what's a girl to do?"

We composed ourselves and went back to Red's little cabin so that I could freshen up and he could change back into his proper clothes. I had truly shocked myself with my behaviour that day. I would never have done anything like that before but Red was my husband now and since we had been together physically he was like an addiction to me. I couldn't get enough of him and I needed to savour every minute possible with him before he departed.

In those last few weeks we talked a lot about being apart from each other. Red promised that he would write to me every day and then post the letter to me at the end of each week and I said I would do the same. This was a poor substitute for the real thing but the best way for me to still feel close to Red every day. I dreaded being apart from him, not only would I miss him but also, I knew our lovely new cottage would feel so lonely without him there. I still had my parents nearby and knew I would have support from Nell and Harry but I knew I would long for Red.

We had a welcome distraction from the countdown when we had Nell and Harry over for dinner one night. They arrived at the door full of smiles and holding hands. It was such a lovely mild evening that Red led them into the garden for a drink whilst I finished off cooking the chops and baby potatoes that we would enjoy for dinner. Nell came into the kitchen grinning and offering to help with the cooking. I said I was fine for help but she could stay in the kitchen with me if she wanted. Nell pulled herself up on to one of the kitchen worktops and curled her fingers round her glass.

"This is a lovely glass, Lily," Nell remarked as she held it up to the light so I would look at her.

I thanked her and then noticed something twinkling coming from one of her fingers. I gasped and ran over to her.

"Nell, oh my, Nell." I burst into joyful tears as I held her hand and looked at her beautiful single diamond ring. "You and Harry are engaged."

Nell nodded at me. I threw my arms up and wrapped them around her. I was so happy for her and so overcome with emotion. I took Nell by the hand and helped her down from the worktop as I rushed into the garden, pulling Nell along with me.

I threw my arms around Harry and kissed him on the cheek as I wished him my congratulations, I looked over at Red who looked perplexed and then I yelled, "They are engaged."

Red's expression changed to sheer joy too and he hugged Nell and then Harry. Red then went into the house and brought out a bottle of sherry as it was a special occasion. We toasted as a four and then Nell came back into the kitchen with me whilst I finished the cooking. I grinned at Nell as I asked her how Harry had proposed.

Nell laughed and said it had been quite unexpected.

"We were up at the top of the lighthouse, shining up the glass on the light," she explained. "I had my dungarees on and my hair piled up high in a rag, I was hardly looking very glamorous. We had just finished one side of the polishing and had sat down on the wooden floor to have our thermos of tea."

I eagerly urged Nell to continue. "We poured the tea out and I had said to Harry how much I love the gleam of the glass on the light when it was freshly polished. We sat looking out at the sea saturated in sunshine with its little white wavy crinkles as far as the eye could see, as we had done many a time before. I placed my head on Harry's shoulder, Harry then said, 'Nell you are the love of my life, my guiding light and my future'. He pulled the ring box out from his pocket and asked me to marry him there and then."

My eyes filled up, it sounded like it had been very romantic and just perfect for Nell. Nell explained how she had said yes instantly and how it meant so much to her that he had asked her in the lighthouse, something so dear to her which was her past and now their present and also their future. We celebrated that night in a haze of merriment and I was so delighted for Nell and Harry, my oldest friends.

In the week before Red was due to set sail, I met up with Nell for lunch. I was pleased to be able to see Nell on her own; it was something we rarely did now as normally Harry and Red would be with us. We got the Rattler into the town and went to Binns. As we entered the grand old façade of the long-standing building, we climbed up the glittery specked stairs to go into the café. I asked Nell if her and Harry had made any wedding plans yet.

Nell beamed. "Yes, we have thought of some things, Lil that I wanted to talk to you about. We want to get married in August and without a doubt we would love you to be our bridesmaid." I smiled back at Nell and was delighted, she continued, "Harry wanted to ask Red to be his best man but he will be away." Nell's face fell. Her and Harry had clearly been worried about this.

"Please don't worry," I said. "It cannot be helped and Red will understand; it is your special day and you should have the wedding when you want to have it."

Nell looked relieved by my words about Red. Nell took my hand then and said, "Are you okay Lil? It's not long until Red goes now, you do know Harry and I will be here for anything you need?"

I was touched by her kindness and I knew that she meant it. I was becoming very emotional of late and I felt a tear ran down my cheek as she wiped it away.

"I am dreading it, Nell. I try and put on a brave face as there are so many other wives in this situation and it is for Red's job and ultimately for our future but I feel like a part of me will be missing."

Nell held both my hands and tried to say something positive to change the subject as she could see it was upsetting me to talk about it. We ate our lunch and turned the chat back to wedding dresses and deciding on a venue for Nell and Harry's wedding reception, which cheered me up.

The days passed by and like a flash it was the day before Red was going to sea. Mine and Red's parents were coming to the cottage for an early fish and chip supper to wish Red well on his voyage. Red welcomed our family into our home as I lightly battered the freshly caught fish and cut the potatoes ready to fry them. Red's mam looked a bit teary; she said she felt like her son was going off to war again. Red hugged her and kept reminding her this was for a job and nothing more. The smell of the sizzling oil filled the house as the food cooked away. When it was ready we all took our plates out to the garden and sat on blankets and took in the summer sunshine. Red and I had not bought a big enough table for everyone to sit but I always think there is something magical about eating fish and chips outside, especially near the beach, where the smell of the sea intersperses with salt and malt vinegar. Red talked about going away. He was nervous and would miss everyone but at the same time he was proud to be taking the completed Ruthy Ann to its new owners who were in Brazil and from there he would be employed as the ship engineer as they transported cargo around South America and the Caribbean, before finally coming back to the UK. The team who worked on the ship really were very skilled and it is such a shame that many of these skills had now been lost to time. We all enjoyed a cup of tea in the garden afterwards before my parents wished Red all the best and left to go home, shortly followed by Red's parents who had more lengthy goodbyes with their son.

Red and I had the rest of the evening with just each other's company; it was what we both wanted. Red helped me tidy up the cottage and then we locked up and went to spend our final night together for a long time. As we got into bed together that night, we tenderly gave ourselves to each other as my body yearned for more. We lay intertwined with our bodies pressing against each other's for the rest of the night. I didn't sleep that night and I don't think Red did much either, we just held each other and I felt sick and in utter turmoil that he was going away. As the dawn broke I knew I only had a few more hours with him; we lay in each other's arms intimately as I embedded every part of him into my mind. The cruel bright sun rose, seeping the room with light as we slowly came to the realisation that we had to get up. I could have stayed there with him forever and never let him go. We embraced once more and then Red showered while I made some breakfast. Red came down the stairs in his new work uniform which was similar to his sailor uniform. He looked very smart and things suddenly became even more real. Neither of us managed to eat as we sipped the tea out of our new wedding cups. Nell and Harry had offered to come with us to the port so that Harry could help with the bags and I think Nell wanted to support me. I knew they would be here soon. I walked over to Red and sat on his knee as we kissed passionately for the last time. The doorbell cut through the silence and it was Nell and Harry. Harry helped Red gather up all the canvas travel bags and we left the cottage. Red turned to look at the cottage when we reached the garden gate and took a deep breath. We all sat quietly on the Rattler journey to the town and then walked slowly down to the port.

The Ruthy Ann stood impressively in the water. She looked even vaster than before, the newly varnished gangway was already receiving the workers, as loved ones bustled at the port side. As we neared the port, I felt ill and I held onto Red and didn't want to let him go. We placed the bags down as Red thanked Harry and hugged him and then hugged Nell and wished them all the best for their wedding. Red and I said our goodbyes, I told him how much I loved him and that I would watch the ship go out to sea from the lighthouse. As we held each other for the final time I gave him a lingering kiss and then Red whispered, "I love you, Lil," in my ear, before turning sharply and going up the gangplank.

As I watched my life, my Red, disappear into the body of the ship, a tear fell down my cheek, as Nell and Harry grabbed both my hands; they were my support now.

We headed back on the Rattler in silence, with Nell stroking my hair as I rested my head on her shoulder. The ship was due to set sail within the next hour and once we got back to Souter, Nell made me a sugary cup of tea as we sat in the lighthouse garden. Nell handed me the well-used pair of binoculars as we saw the majestic Ruthy Ann making her way along the final stretches of the River Tyne to go out to sea. As the ship made the switch from river to sea, her head bobbing up and down, I placed the binoculars up to my eyes and made focus on the ship. There at the front of the ship standing proudly on the deck was Red. He was looking directly at the lighthouse smiling and waving. I quickly jumped up and ran to the edge of the garden and vigorously waved back. I wasn't sure if he would be able to see me but I wanted to wave back. I watched as the ship went further out to sea and I could no longer recognise it. I went back to Nell and Harry who never failed to surprise me.

"Thank you both," I said and hugged them. They had obviously planned this with Red.

Harry walked me home to Honeysuckle. We didn't talk on the walk back but it was a comfort that he was there beside me. As we approached the front door, he watched me unlock it and then he hugged me tightly.

"It will be fine, Lil," Harry said. "Time will go a lot quicker than you think, it always does."

I thanked him again for his help that day and for walking me home. He told me to lock the door and then wave from the window, which I did. I shut the curtains and was alone now in mine and Red's home; the cottage felt empty, as did I. As I made my way upstairs, I crawled into bed and curled up into a ball. I could still smell Red in the huge vacant space that lay next to me, I just wanted him back and he hadn't even been away a night yet, the next few months were going to be hard but I knew I had to be strong for Red. Nevertheless, I still cried myself to sleep that night.

LILY

July 1946

The first week after Red went away felt like an eternity, I had never felt so lonely in my entire life, even though people surrounded me. My job was a saviour for me, it forced me into a routine giving meaning and structure to each day and the smiling happy faces of the children and their ability to learn, diverted me from my own thoughts of life without Red.

The weekend came, and I just wanted to be alone in Honeysuckle. I had a headache and just wanted to lie in my bed staring at the blank ceiling and thinking of Red. I knew this wasn't good for me, but I would allow myself one weekend like this. I knew I wouldn't get a letter from Red this week as it was only the first week but I hoped I might get one soon. I wrote him a paragraph each day just saying what I had been doing and how much I missed him. The next week and weekend came and went. I felt very down and was also starting to worry. I hoped Red was alright, after all, he was on the other side of the world and I had no means to communicate with him. On the Sunday night, I geared myself up for the week that lay ahead; it had been two weeks now and I had not heard from Red. I hoped he had arrived there safely.

The long days felt like they merged into one now. I felt sick with worry. It was Thursday and nearly three weeks since Red left. When I got back to the cottage from school that day, I walked up the path and past the roses which were looking a bit unkempt now and got my key out ready to unlock the door. Something to the left of the door behind the feathery branches of the little purple heather bush caught my eye; it was a small brown parcel. I hurried it up into my arms and scrabbled into the door and locked it behind me. I sat with my back against the door as I tore off the brown paper with its Brazil post mark. Inside, was a letter from Red and a tiny clay statue of Christ the Redeemer. I was overjoyed as I read and reread the letter which started, 'My dearest Lily'.

Red explained how it had been a rough crossing to Brazil with many of the less experienced men becoming quite seasick. It was something they would learn to get used to and it had allowed them all to bond more easily. Once they had reached Brazil they met the new employers who were delighted with their new English cargo ship and seemed to be very fair. Red had seen the imposing statue as they pulled into the Rio docks and had managed to get a little souvenir of it from one of the market stalls near to the docks. He hoped I liked it. The work was long but enjoyable; they were transporting coffee and tobacco from Brazil and steel from Venezuela round to Ecuador and Chile and would be making the journey up north past Venezuela and through the Panama Canal.

I thought it sounded very exciting and tremendously exotic but knew it would be hard work. Red continued in his letter by saying how much he missed me and loved me and was counting down the weeks until he got to see me again. I hugged the letter to my chest along with the little statue which I loved; how thoughtful of him to send me this lovely gift as if I was there with him. The paper had a faint smell of Red's aftershave. I inhaled it deeply as I reread the letter. I slept soundly that night as I knew Red was okay and safe. I put the letter on his pillow that night and the small statue in plain view on the chest of drawers.

The next week passed more quickly. I was able to work more hours at the school on the run up to their summer holidays and I spent a lot of time on evenings and the weekend really starting to clean up the cottage. The gardens became abundant with flowers, a legacy from Mrs Wren and I felt it my duty to tidy up the gardens and tend to the colourful beauties, something which I learnt that I really enjoyed. My mam came and she helped me to really spring clean some of the rooms. We scrubbed away together and I relished having that time with my mam in my own house.

I was greeted on the Monday afternoon by another brown parcel at the front door. I scooped it up and took it into the back garden as it was such a sunny day. The package had an unusual postmark on it – Curacao – I wasn't sure where this was but I was excited to open the parcel. Inside there were two little packages each with a letter, news from my Red. I devoured the contents as my heart skipped a beat to hear from my love. Red had been to Venezuela and they had collected the steel from the port to make the journey round to the other side of South America. He knew that the post would not reach any quicker than from Curacao, so posted the two letters together. The port in Venezuela had been very busy and they had little time there before travelling north to Curacao, which was a small island off the coast of Venezuela, to refuel. Red was missing me deeply and imagined what I would be doing each day. He had only received one of my letters so far, so I knew he must be finding it hard. Red's tone changed in the letter written in Curacao; they had spent two nights docked there and he said what a beautiful island it was with its golden beaches and lagoon-like waters. He described it as paradise and promised me he would take me there one day. I drifted off into a wonderful daydream of me and Red on holiday, our toes in the sand and our skin glowing in the warm sun, until a soft noise moved me abruptly back into the real world as the two little parcels bounced off the grass below me, having fallen off my lap. I had forgotten about them as I read the letters and I opened them. The first was a small painting of Angel Falls which Red attached a note to and had said it was in Venezuela and the biggest waterfall in the world. The second was a miniature glass bottle which was covered in a picture of a sandy beach and palm trees and contained a bright blue liquid. Red had left a note to explain that this was a liqueur and the national drink of Curacao. I was very pleased with these little trinkets and hurried upstairs to put them with my Brazilian statue. I used an old shoe box and covered it in tissue paper and placed my now three letters from Red into it and I placed the precious box next to our bed.

The sun shone brightly over the coastline as it welcomed the month of July. Nell and Harry's wedding was in six weeks' time and gave me something to focus on and look forward to. In the last week before the school finished for the holiday, I received another parcel from Red. I had started to really look forward to the extra item he would send along with the letter; it heartened me to think that in the business of his job he still found the time to add a precious extra with my letter. The next letter came in a small brown box and detailed Red's journey as he went through the Panama Canal and its intricate locking system. Red had made good friends with one of the other engineers who was also newly married, so I was pleased he had someone out there with him going through the same thing. The box contained six colourful coasters with a photo of the Panama Canal on. They would come in very handy. I put five of them in the kitchen cupboard to be used and I placed one next to my other items.

The school finished for its summer holidays and suddenly I had a lot more time on my hands, so I was able to help Nell with the wedding. Nell wanted to have green as the colour for her wedding as an ode to her maiden name, which I thought was a lovely gesture. I went with Nell to pick her dress and also a green dress for myself and she picked green ties and handkerchiefs for the wedding party. The wedding was to take place in the same church as Red and I had got married but the reception would be in The Grand which was a lovely old house in Whitburn which had recently been converted into a hotel. Always one to push boundaries, Nell had asked whether I would feel comfortable doing a reading at the reception for her and Harry. Harry had asked his father to be best man but she felt I should be involved in the day as a stand in voice for Red. I gladly accepted and asked if I could write her a poem, as her and Harry and made our day so very wonderful.

It was two weeks before the wedding; Nell was getting a cake made and we had been trying out the different flavours for her to choose from. On the way back from the town I invited Nell back to the cottage for a cup of tea.

When we got to the cottage there was a new parcel waiting for me and I took it into the kitchen and opened it whilst I made the tea. I put the letters to one side to read alone once Nell had gone and I opened up the two smaller packages. The first was a colourful red bird ornament. It was beautiful and under its cylinder base it read 'Ecuador - Hummingbird'. The second was a more curious looking ornament which was a small grey long head; at this base it said 'Easter Island'. I showed Nell the two objects and placed them on the kitchen bench. All of a sudden, I began to feel quite faint and I lost my footing as Nell caught me and then assisted me carefully over to the chair. I had never gone light-headed like this before and wondered if it might have been from all the cake. Nell looked worried and said she would take me to the doctor in the morning.

I went to bed that night lonely. I read the words of the new letter and I missed Red so much. He detailed how he had only really seen the ports in Ecuador and Chile but heard about the Easter Island heads from some of the locals. After Ecuador, the Ruthy Ann would voyage back up through Panama and then through to the Caribbean to collect a variety of cargo to take to Greenland, Iceland and then the US. As I lay on the bed absorbing the letter, I thought more about Red, then it suddenly hit me. In the midst of Red going to sea and the planning around it, I realised I was late. My last time which I could remember properly was before the wedding as I was so relieved it was before I had to wear a white dress. I suddenly realised there was every chance I could be pregnant and it would explain some of the headaches and tiredness which I thought were from being apart from Red and it would really explain my dizzy episode.

Nell came to the cottage early the next morning to come with me to the doctors. As I opened the door to her I smiled at her nervously.

"Come in, Nell," I said. "I think I know what is wrong. I don't think I am ill but I think I am pregnant."

Nell clasped her hands to her mouth.

"Oh, Lily," she cried as she hugged me carefully.

"I think I must still be quite early but it would certainly explain a lot," I said.

Nell took my hand as we went to the doctor together in Whitburn. When we got to the surgery we took a seat and waited anxiously until my name was called. Nell squeezed my hand as I went in to see the doctor alone. The doctor asked me about my symptoms and when my last period was and then asked me to lie down as she felt my tummy. The conclusion was positive and as my tummy had hardened somewhat she thought I could be anywhere between 9-12 weeks but time would tell. She also explained that it was common to get a little dizzy at times and to try and rest. In those days there was no access to pregnancy tests or hospital appointments, so you were very much left in the dark over timings. I thanked the doctor and as I left her room a smile spread across my face, I was going to be a mammy and Red and I were going to have a baby. Nell knew as soon as she saw my face that it was good news.

It was one week before Nell and Harry's wedding and I was getting excited for the day. I had continued to write to Red but decided not to tell him about the pregnancy yet as it still felt very early. I felt like I was starting to get a tiny bump as if I had eaten a humongous lunch. Luckily, I still fit into my bridesmaid dress without drawing any attention to my waist. Nell had promised not to say anything about my pregnancy, not even to Harry, as I didn't want to tempt fate.

The parcel that arrived from Red that week confirmed my suspicions. A letter from Panama was attached to a flat white cloth item which Red said was a hat. I placed it on my head and it smelled of Red. I inhaled the scent deeply as I placed my hands on the precious cargo inside of me. The second letter detailed Red's arrival in Cuba, which he described as humid and bright with all of its colourful houses and colourful cars. They were collecting coffee there to take north. He said how the music was fantastic over there and that Nell and Harry would really appreciate it and the locals danced together in a very sensual manner. I drifted off again happily, as I imagined me and Red dancing together sensually before I came back to reality. I opened the second package and it was a little jar of coffee. I took the lid off to smell it and I promptly ran to the toilet and vomited with my hat still on my head. I could not stand the smell of the coffee, I was pretty sure I was pregnant before but now I knew it. I cleaned myself up and put the hat with my other treasures from Red but I put the coffee in a drawer in the small bedroom, far out of my view for now.

The day of Nell and Harry's wedding arrived and I wore my green dress and I felt so proud of them both. That night, when I got into bed I wrote about it in my letter to Red.

'My dearest Red,
Today was Nell and Harry's wedding, it really was the most perfect day for them. Nell looked radiant in her white gown and Harry so smart in his suit. Nell picked green as her colour and had the church door decorated with green bunting. They hired a bus to take us all to The Grand in Whitburn and they hired a lovely green wedding car for their journey. The reception went really well and Harry mentioned you in his speech which made me miss you even more. You would have loved it and you were really a big miss on the day. I read out my poem as I said I would and I have written my final copy out for you to read, I hope you like it.

The Lighthouse

You stand before me, my focal point in a widespread landscape.
You stand beyond me, my light in a bitter darkness.
You stand behind me, my guide in those hazy days.
You stand beside me, my protector against the elements.
You stand below me, my foundation in life.
You stand by me, my love, always.

I am counting down the days until you get home. I was so happy today
but it really made me miss my wonderful husband even more.

All my love forever,
Lily

The leaves in the garden began to fall marking the beginning of autumn, it was probably my favourite season. I used to love walking through the golden fallen leaves, kicking them up as I went. The air turned crisper, marking the beginning of blazes in the fireplaces, woollen hats and scarves and thick hot broth. My mam would make her chicken broth with barley, lentils and root vegetables and you used to be able to smell it cooking away as you got near the terrace. What I wouldn't give to have a bowl of that broth now. My tummy had swelled and I had a little bump now to keep me company; a constant reminder of my love for Red. My parents knew that I was pregnant now and were overjoyed by the news but I still didn't want to tell anyone else as I still felt cautious. I decided to continue with my work in the school as I found that it was manageable for me now with it being three days a week but I did tell the headmistress my news in confidence and we decided I would work up until Christmas. I would then need to speak to Red about the future but I knew I did eventually want to work again. I received my next letter from Red in the second week of September. It had a Jamaican post mark on it and inside was my precious letter and a small ornament of a palm tree. Red explained how they were collecting rum in Jamaica before stopping at the Dominican Republic. Red said Jamaica looked like a beautiful place but there was violence in the port, so he was glad they were not staying there. I worried about Red that night as I reread my letter and looked at my growing collection of treasures on the dressing table.

The last week of September came and my bump was beginning to get more pronounced. I must have been about 16-19 weeks now and I was starting to feel funny things in my tummy, as if tiny bubbles were floating along the inside of my skin. It was a lovely feeling. Nell and Harry got great news this week too; they had been living with Nell's parents in the lighthouse cottage whilst they decided what to do. As they were both learning the lighthouse keeper's trade they ideally needed to live in the lighthouse cottages or very nearby but none of the cottages were available. However, this changed when the eldest lighthouse keeper announced he was due to retire which would mean a cottage would be available at the end of October. Nell and Harry were overjoyed and could not wait to have a home they could call their own. My final parcel in September arrived this week and it was from the Dominican Republic. I opened it up and the letter was paired with a smiley grey donkey wearing a yellow hat. I laughed, he was great. Red had said that they were collecting thousands upon thousands of bananas in the Dominican. Red explained that the port there was busy and the buildings very beautiful but that poverty was hidden amongst them. All the locals seemed very happy however and drank coffee and danced the local dance 'the merengue' without a care in the world. The weather was very hot there and the tiny cabins in the Ruthy Ann had become stifling at times so Red was looking forward to travelling north to cooler climates. I hugged the letter to my chest on the last day in September which marked half way down, less than three months to go before Red was home and also five months or so until he became a father.

October came and the winds that came from the sea began to get colder. I had got into a routine with my parents on a Sunday now, where I would go through to their house and have lunch with them. My mam would wear her pinny and serve up meat, vegetables, Yorkshire pudding and crackling. It was something I would truly look forward to at the end of the week, wonderful home-cooked food and spending time with my parents in my old home. People in the village knew about my pregnancy now and I had also separately told Red's parents but told them I wanted to surprise him when he got home, he would only worry intensely about me while he was away.

The children at school were excited by my bump and Nell had started popping out of the lighthouse at three p.m. to accompany me on the five-minute walk back to Honeysuckle. It was very kind of her to do this even though I urged her I would be okay. Nell would come in and have a cup of tea and call it her lunch break, it was nice to have the time with her. We got back one afternoon and a parcel was waiting for me from my Red. This time the parcel had a Greenland postmark on it. Red had really been able to visit some fantastic places. I opened it up and the letter detailed how the ship was making deliveries in Greenland and then Iceland before it would go to the US and then back to Europe where it would change staff and voyage round Europe and Africa. The parcel contained a small colourful lovely-looking yellow house, almost like a toy house, Red explained how this was what the houses looked like there and from the distance of the ship they looked like tiny jewels dotted across the landscape. I imagined it must be wonderful living in one of those little houses.

Nell then inspected the small yellow house and suddenly laughed. "Lil, I forgot to tell you, we get the keys to Keepers Cottage 3 next week."

I was pleased that everything had worked out for them and that they would be so near.

"I can't wait to come around," I replied to Nell with a laugh.

The weather began to cool as the end of October drew near. I really enjoyed getting back into the cottage and putting the fire on and sitting down on the sofa wrapping myself in a blanket with a mug of my mam's proper broth, which she was kindly churning out for me. To this day, I still think there is something thrilling about being so warm and cosy yet looking out at the chilly weather soaring over the sea. My bump had really begun to grow now and on the day my last parcel in October came, with an Icelandic post mark, I opened it up to reveal my letter from Red which was full of words of love and hopes for our future and also a small white whale ornament. I suddenly felt a proper kick in my abdomen, the most miraculous feeling of my life. My baby was really moving about now. I like to think that because I was so happy with my letter from Red, my happiness was released and felt by our baby. I could not wait for Red to be home to be able to share this excitement.

ANNA

May 2017

Two weeks had passed and James and I made the train journey again back to London for Nora's and Tim's wedding. I really hoped that it would be a nice wedding for them and that they would be happy together. Nora had failed to invite any of my family to her wedding even though she had known them for most of her life and they had watched her grow up, something which left a somewhat bitter taste in my mouth.

The wedding was to take place on the Saturday followed by a restful Sunday in London and then James and I would travel back up North, home, on the Monday. On the Friday evening, James and I went to dinner. Recently, we had not spoken much about the job offer or our own wedding and we needed to make a final decision about both. I had decided that I would meet with Al, my ultimate boss, again on the Monday following the wedding, to give him my final decision on his time-lapsed offer. As I sat opposite my handsome fiancé in a quaint little Greek restaurant, in the middle of London, I tried to gauge his true feelings towards the job opportunity.

"It would be a great step up for my career and the money would be a huge help. Think of what we might be able to do with that extra money," I said to James, exploring the detail of his manly face.

"You don't need to convince me Anna, it has to be your choice and your choice alone. I have already said I will support you whatever you decide. It's not a long-term thing so it's whether you want to do it and push yourself," James responded.

I must admit, the longer hours and time away from my family did worry me; an untradeable commodity and something that no amount of money could buy. I knew I had to decide soon but thought I would enjoy the weekend and the solution I was sure, would come to me by Monday and I knew it was a decision that I had to make myself.

I had spent the Saturday morning getting ready for Tim and Nora's wedding and having known that it would be a very smart affair I had decided to wear a full length violet-coloured dress, whilst James would wear a tuxedo. I applied my make-up carefully in the dim hue of the small hotel bathroom light and then proceeded to curl my hair using a chopstick curler wand. I could hear James in the background rustling about as he struggled with his bow tie.

"Anna," he called in desperation.

"On it," I chirped, as I rushed over to him with a mane of hair on one side and straight unruly hair on the other.

"My god, you are a gorgeous creature," James said as he put his hands around my waist and pulled me towards him. "Some days I still can't get over that one day you will be my wife!" he said.

I laughed and gave him a quick kiss then moved his hands. "You will smudge my make-up. Here, give me your tie," I told him. I delicately sorted out the tie and wrapped it carefully around my beloved's neck, as he turned around to face me showing himself off in his full tuxedo. I grinned and pulled him in to me and stated, "I think I am the lucky one, Mr Thompson."

We both giggled, finished getting glammed up and then composed ourselves to make our way down to the hotel foyer and to order a taxi to get to Sinton Hall.

I knew Sinton Hall would be grand but as the black cab pulled into its walled park-like surroundings, I could not believe that we were still in the built-up London city. The grounds were truly beautiful with lush freshly cut green lawns which were divided up by carefully cut boxy hedgerows which were then further separated out by row upon row of wild blooms who peaked out charmingly from under them. It reminded me so much of the vastness of the North East and again I had to wonder why Nora had picked to have her wedding in a city in which she did not use the city as a backdrop.

As James and I strode up the stone stairs and into the foyer of the hall, we were taken aback by the number of people we could see milling around the reception area of this great hall. Surely not everyone could be here for the wedding? There must have been over three hundred people. James nudged me as a young chap in a suit and apron quickly galloped over to us with a tray of champagne. We both took a glass as the young chap galloped off to his next arrivals.

James leant over to me and muttered, "I don't think I even know three hundred people, who are all of these people?"

I shrugged and took a big gulp of my bubbly. As we meandered around some of the huge columns in the reception hall and in and out the many people, we stumbled across Jo, Kate and Zoe and their partners, I was glad to see some friendly faces, I had not seen any of Nora's family yet.

As I hugged the girls, they all had the same question, 'Who are all these people?' They certainly were not from Nora's side, so we presumed they must be from Tim's. A loud bell then rang and an announcement was made that we must take our seats in the mirrored room for the wedding ceremony. As James and I entered the mirrored room, the room was exactly as described: floor to ceiling mirrors and Nora had arranged for rose petals to be scattered up and down the aisle. I looked upon the row and row of people and became very sad. There on the front row was Tim's family and sitting proudly was what must have been his grandparents. I felt awful for Nora's Nanna, Pops and her Great Aunt Ida and I became really angry with Nora. How could she have been so heartless as to exclude them from such an event which would clearly have meant so much to them? As I scanned the rows further I still could not see other members of Nora's family and I wondered if it was only going to be Nora's parents who would be in attendance.

Tim entered the room with his ushers and the throngs of people became quiet, a few minutes passed and then the officiant asked for silence as the twelve musicians who made up a triple string quartet began to play their beautiful tones to mark the entrance of the wedding party. Nora's mam walked down the aisle first and she looked lovely but also rather tense. She was followed by Sarah, Tim's sister, who sashayed down the aisle in her designer gown with what I can only describe as a smug look. It still really hurt me that Nora, who was supposed to be my childhood friend and also my own bridesmaid, had excluded me so much from her big celebration. I was merely a guest to her, whereas I always viewed her as my closest friend. I had learnt this now. The triple quartet then started a new tune and Nora and her father made their entrance into the mirrored room and up the aisle. Nora did look radiant in her jewel-encrusted vintage-looking gown which swept the aisle and the petals as she moved but she also looked painfully thin. I felt sad for her that she had put so much pressure on herself to lose so much weight.

The ceremony went by and was over in fifteen minutes, by which point Tim and Nora were married. They both looked very happy as the guests made their way back into the reception hall and then out into the grounds of Sinton Hall where canapés and further champagne flowed freely. I could overhear some of the guests and they were all talking about business and deals they had done recently. I found this very odd and somewhat rude, surely, they should be talking about the marriage and start of a new chapter of the couple whose wedding they had just witnessed. James and I stood with the girls and their partners until we were summoned into the banqueting hall for the wedding breakfast. The hugely tiered hand-painted cake was on display as we entered, with a logo for T and N painted all over it. As the guests all took their seats it became apparent that most of the guests were Tim's father's business associates and he worked the room, networking from table to table. I started to feel a bit sorry for Nora. The wedding breakfast was very nice, and the speeches were done quickly, I felt very bad for Nora's dad who looked so nervous speaking in front of so many people but he did Nora and her mam proud and Nora looked delighted with his words and showed glimpses of her old self again as he spoke.

James and I managed to see Nora's parents in the lull after the meal whilst Nora and Tim were having photos taken.

"Congratulations to you both," I said, as I hugged them both.

Nora's mam hugged me back. "I am so glad you came, Anna. A familiar face."

I didn't want to mention about Nora's grandparents or Great Aunt but Nora's mam brought them up. "More of the family would have loved to see Nora married but so many couldn't travel and they couldn't get babysitters," Nora's mam explained.

I didn't know what to say. I just smiled back and said, "It's a beautiful wedding and Nora looks happy."

Nora's parents were then summoned away for photos. I looked at James and he knew I felt so upset for Nora's family.

The day became night and the evening merriment started with the state rooms being opened up. The first room was set up with all of the virtual racing games and a roulette table with croupier and the second room was set up with various stands giving out the wedding favours which, as had been promised, ranged from charm bracelets for the ladies, cufflinks for the men, T and N embossed champagne bottles, T and N embossed scented candles and T and N embossed floral soaps. James nudged me again as we looked around. I knew what he was thinking: it was all a bit much. The conservatory room was then opened and guests ushered into it, to mark the start of the band and first dance. The band were very good and talented musicians and singers as they belted out Motown songs. Nora and Tim looked happy and relaxed now and we managed to speak to them briefly on the dance floor before they were ushered off by Tim's father to meet some other people. As the evening approached midnight, I was starting to get tired and ready to head back to the hotel soon but I knew there was still one surprise to go, the midnight firework display. At eleven forty-five p.m. the guests were ushered back out onto the hall lawns whilst flash upon flash of bright lights and colours whizzed across the sky in front of us. I liked the fireworks but couldn't help but think the children in Nora's family would have loved it even more.

James and I said our goodbyes and made our way back to our hotel where we collapsed on our bed in giggles, overwhelmed by the extravagance of everything. James had fallen asleep very quickly and as I lay next to him I reached a very contemplative mood. I was glad that Nora and Tim were married and that they looked like they had enjoyed their wedding day but I also felt very sad for them. The most important aspect of their day, the ceremony of marriage, was over in fifteen minutes and then the day was treated like a business networking event for Tim's father, rather than it being a celebration of two people dedicating their lives to one another. As I lay in my hotel bed awake I thought increasingly about what makes a wedding and I concluded that it is not how much money you can spend or what things you have at the wedding but more so the meaning of marriage and the people who are there to watch you make those sacred vows. As I thought about Nora's family and how clearly disappointed her parents were by her decision to exclude her family from her life, I decided myself, there and then about Al's job offer.

My thoughts then wandered to my gran and what she would have made of Nora's wedding today and how detached mine and Nora's friendship had become. I couldn't help but think that my gran, with her strong belief in love, would have found today's wedding somewhat lacking and would have been confused about where the celebration of love, family and friendship was in the occasion which took place today.

LILY

November 1946

N ell and Harry had finally moved into their marital cottage and I was really looking forward to visiting them in their own home. I had, of course, offered to help them but Harry and Nell were having absolutely none of it. I had taken up knitting again, a pastime that I found quite relaxing, since I knew I was expecting and I decided to knit and create Nell and Harry a throw with a small scene of the lighthouse with seabirds flying around it and a couple sitting on a bench. I hoped they liked it. They could use it on one of their chairs or as a blanket. I was going to take it over to them and finally see their cottage in its full glory. I had spent the morning baking and had rustled up some homemade fruit scones to take too when a knock on the door interrupted my packing of the baked goods. I curiously creaked open the door to the cheery face of the postman who had a letter for me which I had to sign for. It had an Icelandic postmark. I was really starting to worry. I had already received an Iceland letter from Red. I signed for the package, politely thanked the postman and then stood, panicked, behind my front door as I frantically tore open the letter. As I absorbed the contents, I squealed with delight. I hurriedly put the scones in some brown paper, grabbed the throw which I had wrapped in a ribbon and quickly threw my winter coat on, to make the short walk over to Nell and Harry's cottage.

The newly painted pale green cottage door opened and Harry and Nell welcomed me in, Harry's arm draped over Nell's shoulders protectively. "Come in, Lil and welcome," said Harry as he ushered me in with his arm proudly. Nell took my hand excitedly as she showed me around each of the carefully thought out rooms which complimented their joint love of the sea and Nell's love of the seabirds.

"What do you think, Lil?" she said, eagerly waiting for my answer.

"I just love it. It is so perfect for you both and Nell, it is wonderful how you have made it so homely in such a short space of time," I explained.

I really was very impressed with how hard they both must have worked to get the cottage like this.

"I made these for you both," I said, as I handed Nell the throw and Harry the scones.

Nell opened the throw and saw the lighthouse. "Lil," she gasped. 'This is just wonderful and so personal, thank you so much," as she then carefully placed it over her old rocking chair in the living room.

"Come," Nell said, as she led me to the light-blue-coloured kitchen with Harry. "I have made a fresh pot of tea for us."

We all took our seats round the worn wooden table, on which in the middle of it Nell had placed a blue candle on a doily. As I sat down and looked out the window, the views from the cottage were truly enchanting. The red and white striped lighthouse stood out boldly in front of its blue backdrop with our lovely little village sitting securely behind it. I took a sip of the hot tea that Nell had poured and let the hot liquid trickle down the back of my throat. Suddenly the baby kicked again. I took Nell's hand.

"Quick, feel this," I said, giggling "The baby must like the tea."

Harry placed his hand next to Nell's and they both looked at me with astonishment.

"Lily, that is remarkable. The baby is saying hello. Red is going to be absolutely captivated when he gets back," Harry said.

I smiled at them both. "Actually, speaking of Red, I just got the most incredible news from him," I exclaimed.

"I got another letter from Iceland today. Red is coming back a month earlier than planned," I yelled with joy. "The shipping company decided that instead of them going back to the US they would take the ship to Scandinavia to deliver the last of the coffee and bananas there. Then they would pick up additional cargo to deliver into the UK before docking in Southampton to change staff, where Red will finish this work project and be able to get the train home."

I saw the smiles form on Nell and Harry's faces. I continued. "Guess where they will be doing the UK delivery?" I screeched with excitement. "The Tyne. The deliveries are for the North of England and parts of Scotland."

I was so happy. I knew I would not actually get to physically see Red for the delivery but it did mean that I would be able to see the ship coming into the Port and that if I used Nell's dad's binoculars again I might be able to catch a glimpse of him. Harry and Nell were delighted for me and also really excited themselves to see Red again and earlier than planned and I couldn't wait for him to learn about our life-changing news.

The baby was really moving about at pace now. I calculated I must have been around about five months pregnant. My bump was blooming and the baby allowed me to feel a real closeness with Red; even though oceans separated us, we now had an unbreakable bond and I couldn't wait for us to be a family.

In his second letter from Iceland, Red had said that the Ruthy Ann would be docking in the Tyne on the 27th November before making her final way down to Southampton and Red would get the train back up the coast to mark the final part of the journey back up to the North East on the 30th November. I could barely contain my excitement and was now on an official countdown until Red was home.

The 9th of November came and marked three weeks until I would see Red again and on this day I received one of his thoughtful packages. In this package was a small Viking ornament with a hairy long beard. It made me laugh as Red had picked a Viking with red hair. I wondered to myself if Red had grown a beard like this whilst he was away. I could faintly smell Red's aftershave on the letter and longed to be reunited with him and to smell that woody scent in its full glory. Red explained how he liked Sweden and commented on how clean and unspoilt it was. They managed to unload a lot of the cargo there with the final delivery of cargo being in Norway in the next few days.

To keep myself occupied and my mind more restful, on the days where I was not working in the school, I spent my time with my mam knitting some items for the baby. I reckoned that the baby would arrive in late February or early March, so the weather would still be cool. It was really nice to be able to go back to the terrace and sit with my mam in the small cosy kitchen as we knitted away together. My dad still worked hard and some days I would help my mam make the dinner for my dad, all the pots cooking and boiling away merrily together on the worn black stove. My mam had begun to make pan haggerty again to mark the winter months and my dad used to come back frozen to the bone and ready for his hot meal. I used to stay for dinner frequently and I would secretly watch them together and how they still loved each other so much after all this time. They had brought me up so well and I knew and respected the importance of family, something which I wanted to replicate for my own growing family.

The following week, with just fifteen days to go until Red was home, I received my next parcel which had a Norwegian post mark. Part of me actually started to feel a little bit sad that this might be my last parcel from Red. I had really come to look forward to the loving words and quaint surprises, however they failed in comparison to the real thing. I could not wait to wrap my arms around him and run my fingers through that russet hair and that smile, his beautiful smile. I really could not wait to see that and his reaction to my bump. I opened the parcel and the letter from Red. Red had passed through some large masses of water to get to the port in Norway, he said these were called fjords and he said it was the most incredible scenery and looked almost unearthly. The water was so crystal clear that the mountains, with their green spiny pine trees, would reflect in the mirror-like waters below them. He said it was almost like looking at two separate worlds which met in the middle and he was lucky enough to look into both. Red said that they managed to enjoy a meal in one of the local restaurants and the fish that was served was freshly caught hours beforehand. It reminded him so much of home and he could not wait to get back. I opened up the small package which was attached to the letter; it was a glass square and inside was a scene of a fjord surrounded by mountains. I placed it on the old dresser with my other items which had amassed to quite a fruitful collection now. I felt so proud of Red that he had been able to experience all of these places with his work. I put the letter in the box and I slept well that night. I dreamt of Red and him and I laughing with a little girl in the garden, weaving in and out of the roses. I wondered if this meant something.

The days became shorter as the end of the month became nearer. It was the 25th of November now and only five days until I would be reunited with my husband. The baby was kicking away now and my bump was somewhat rounded.

It was a funny feeling going about my daily life with my new friend in my tummy to keep me company; daily life was normal but what I was creating was extraordinary. To my surprise, I received another brown parcel, this time with a Danish postmark. I didn't think I would get another letter off Red before I would see him; this would definitely be the last one.

I carefully opened up the parcel and in the letter Red explained how they had loaded the ship with mountains of butter and bacon in Denmark which would be delivered to the UK. He was really looking forward to the first stop to just be able to see his beloved North East again. He would look out at Souter and knew that all his family would be nearby and then we would be properly reunited shortly afterwards. Red explained that this was something which was keeping him going and made the days seem shorter. Red liked Denmark and again remarked on how clean it was and how much he had enjoyed the freshly baked plaited salt speckled bread which was widely available at the port. I opened up the parcel to reveal my final curiosity which Red had chosen for me. It was a beautiful dainty ornament of a lonesome little mermaid sitting on a rock and looking out to sea. He left a note with it and said it reminded him of me and Marsden Rock looking out to sea for him. I laughed at this notion as I had a vision of myself lounging on the rock looking out to sea. I felt a bond with this lonely mermaid and I wondered who her great love was and who she was waiting for. I too was lonely but I was also lucky, I knew exactly who I was waiting for and I couldn't wait to hold him in my arms again.

LILY

27th November 1946

I woke up feeling refreshed that morning and ready for the day which lay ahead of me. I knew I wouldn't be able to be near Red or speak to him but I would be able to look from afar and that was more than enough for me today.

I lovingly cradled my bump and murmured sweetly to it under my smile, "You will get to see Daddy today." It really had been a long five months apart from Red; I was going to head to the lighthouse to have a homemade lunch with Harry and Nell and then watch for the Ruthy Ann coming into port around three p.m. I felt so full of pride that Red would be coming back into the Tyne port in a ship that he himself had helped build.

I got myself ready and wrapped up warm and I took some time to myself to reread all my letters from Red and to look at my wonderful collection of treasures from his journey. I looked out of the window and the sky looked a bit grey and it was raining lightly. I groaned to myself as I had hoped it would be a dry day, so I would get the clearest possible view of the ship coming in. I put on my winter coat and gloves and I locked the house and made the short walk over to the lighthouse cottage.

Nell greeted me at the door. "Come on, Lil," said Nell, pulling me in. "Let's get you in out of this cold," as she ushered me into the main room with its crackling coal burning fire.

"Where is Harry?" I said, as I turned my head to look around to search him out. In that very same moment the room was immersed in a loud blast as the lighthouse foghorn went off. I then turned my body to look out of the window again as mist started to engulf the cliffs, a mist so dense that it blinded the view of the village from the window.

"Oh no," I wailed, as I worried I would not be able to see the ship. Harry came in the door panting and looked at Nell.

Nell tried to calm me. "It is most likely just a sea fret, Lil, and it will pass," she said, but I could tell from their concerned glances at each other that she was only trying to be kind and having lived by the sea all my life, I knew this fog could last for hours.

Harry went back out to assist Mr Green as they shone the beam out from the heart of Souter, as it outstretched its light like tentacles deep into the fog.

Nell poured me a cup of tea and looked at my disappointed face.

"It still might clear," she said encouragingly. "We can go to the landing in the lighthouse if not, and we might still be able to see the ship."

I smiled at her as I sipped my tea. Nell always could calm me and she was right, the window in the landing was one level down from the beam and I might be able to see the ship from above the fog but Red would not be able to see me. At one p.m. Harry came back in and we ate a light lunch together, one of Nell's meat pies. The rain was starting to lash down onto the cottage windows by this point and I could hear the wind whistling and gaining momentum; it dawned on me that the sea would be rough. I knew Red was an accomplished sailor but I still worried about him in the ship. Time ticked on slowly and by two p.m., the wind had worsened. Nell carefully led me and my bump into the lighthouse and up those spiral stairs which I had climbed many a time before, as we finally got to the landing room with its panoramic window and her father's trusty binoculars.

We sat; I twiddled my thumbs; I counted the panels of the floorboards and we waited and waited. Nell held my hand, which was a comfort. The clock got to 2.40 p.m. and by this point, the callous wind had moved the feeble fog on, cackling as it went but what it brought with it was a demon beyond imagination. In the not too far distance, the sky had darkened, thick black sooty clouds were advancing to the meagre cliffs and towards us, belting out flashes of fire as they went. I was frightened and I held my bump. I had never seen a storm like this before. I hoped that the Ruthy Ann was either running late or even better, had not even left Denmark yet. I clung to this thought of hope, until my heart sank.

In the distance I could see the faint outline of a ship advancing towards us. I knew before picking up the binoculars it would be the Ruthy Ann and on it would be the core of my entire life. From one side of the lighthouse I could see the ship approaching as it veered in and out of the vast waves which tossed it from side to side. I held my breath each time it dipped down into the cavernous seas, before it skilfully reappeared. I didn't want to take my eyes off the ship but from the corner of my eye, I knew that the dark skies were coming nearer and nearer. I could see Harry out the window frantically working away by the foghorn, his overalls completely soaked through and desperately sounding the horn at specific intervals. The rain spat and lashed around the lighthouse like a vortex as if the lighthouse had become captured by the storm. I desperately scrutinised the sea line with the binoculars as the storm pounded the coastline and proceeded to make its unforgiving way towards the ship.

As I watched intensely, there was suddenly a flash of light and an almighty clash and the lighthouse fell into a gloomy darkness. I could hear the usually docile Mr Green screaming at the top of his voice at Nell and Harry now and I felt scared. "The power's been hit. Get in the engine room now, we have to get the second generator on." I could hear them frantically moving about below me; I felt helpless and small, I didn't know what to do or how I could help them. I huddled myself into a ball as I cried and focussed myself on the only thing I could: watching the ship.

The sea was sunk into complete blackness for what must have only been a minute, but to me it felt like an eternity. I needed to be able to see the Ruthy Ann and I needed to make sure my Red was okay. The lights swiftly came back on in the lighthouse which distracted me for a moment, as the beam radiated across the sea again. When I was able to regain focus on the ship, I felt a sharp pain in my chest as I screamed and then vomited across the landing room floorboard. One of the grand wooden masts on the main deck of the ship had been struck by lightning and was distressingly ablaze. I could see the crew running about like tiny ants trying to steady the ship as the mast fell sideways across the ship setting the deck with its varnished wooden pathways on fire. The wind howled with a wispy malevolent laugh and the now shadowy dark sky roared with retaliation as they argued amongst themselves. I ran down the small circular lighthouse steps one by one, binoculars in hand, and made my way out through the heavy lighthouse back door and into the sodden allotments towards the edge of the cliff. The rain thrashed violently down on my skin and soaked through my clothes but I didn't feel anything. I held the faithful binoculars closely up to my face and desperately wiped them down with my sleeve.

I peered through the binoculars, terrified, as I could see that the ship was losing control now and was starting to drift in the direction of the lighthouse and the danger of the cliffs. The deck was still alight and I could see that the crew were lowering the lifeboats into the water one by one. I saw Red then, my heart pounded and I felt as if this wasn't really happening to me, it was someone else's nightmare which I was just watching from afar. Along with three other crew members I could see that Red was pushing the rest of the crew into the boats. What was he doing? Why wasn't he getting in too? I yelled and screamed and pleaded with him to get into a boat but I knew he couldn't hear me. Hot sticky tears stuck to my face as I continued to watch in horror as Red and his three colleagues gathered up the last remaining crew and pushed them into the last lifeboat and towards the safety of the land in the bay. The other three sailors dived into the perilous black sea and then I watched Red and saw his face turn to sheer panic as he took one last glance at the Ruthy

Ann and the flames which overwhelmed it, a final look up at Souter Lighthouse and then, with no further hesitation, dived into the sea.

I dropped the binoculars as I felt my knees hit the wet soil underneath me and as I painfully screamed into the palms of my clenched fists.

I don't know how long I was on the ground for but I could feel a presence behind me, it was Harry. I grabbed him and shrieked at him, "He jumped in, Red jumped into the water."

Harry took one look at me as he then scooped me up, lifted me and took me back up to the lighthouse.

I was hysterical at this point and was not making any sense at all. Harry screeched for Nell as he took me through the door. He muttered something to Nell whose face froze as he ran out the door again and into the village. By this point I thought I was dreaming, it wasn't real; I was meant to see Red today and it would be a lovely day. I would wake up soon and everything would be fine and as it should be.

The baby proceeded to kick me back into reality. It really wasn't fine at all. I sobbed into Nell's arms as I saw my mam run through the door, her golden hair flowing wildly from the storm. My mam gathered me in her arms as she said words which I barely understood to Nell: "Nell, the men from the village have gone down to Fisherman's Cove. The lifeboats are coming in there. Mick and Harry have gone with them. You get back to work in the lighthouse. I will take Lily to the village."

I was in total shock by this point. I don't know how I physically got back to the terrace but my mam got me there using all her strength. The wind still howled through the village raging at our clothes as the rain lashed down onto our skin. It was evening now and the sea looked like murky oil. I wanted to go down to the cove too. I pleaded and begged with my mam with all my might to let me but she was firm with her words as she said, "Lily, you are pregnant, this is not the time for you to be going. Your dad and Harry said they would search the cove for Red until nightfall."

I knew she was right. I then felt ill and threw up again in sheer frustration and shock as she made me sit on the chair in the kitchen sipping hot sugary black tea, before sending me up to lie on my old bed.

I must have passed out at some point with exhaustion from what was going on but at midnight I heard the deep muffled tone of male voices. I rushed downstairs in hope, my dad and Harry had come into the terrace. I could hear them whispering; I hoped and dreamed it would be something positive. I learnt that the other three sailors who had dived in had reached the cove. Two were taken straight to hospital but seemed to be not terribly hurt, whereas the third sailor had been thrown against the cliff and was taken to hospital in a bad way. My mam saw me loitering and gripped me and shook her head at me. I collapsed to the floor. Red was a strong swimmer, why hadn't he come to shore behind the others? Why hadn't he got into one of the boats?

I tried to run past my family and out the front door of the terrace but my dad got a strong hold of me. "Don't be mad, Lily, it's pitch black and unsafe now," he said as he held me in his protective arms.

As I sobbed into my dad's chest, I saw a solitary tear run down his wind-battered face as he softly said, "We can go back as soon as light breaks."

I lay on my old bed that night tormenting myself as I counted down the minutes, pleading and bargaining with the sun to rise earlier that day. I didn't understand what had happened and how it could have happened but I needed to look for Red. I just needed there to be light.

ANNA

June 2017

As I looked out to the sea on a sunny June morning and I saw the sunlight shimmering in beams off the crested waters, I casually sipped my cup of tea and I knew there and then that I had made the right decision in turning down the job offer in London.

As I reflected on my decision, I thought how, in my view, there is no better place on earth than the North East of England and why would I want to leave what is on my doorstep and my home for a lonely and long working week in a vast and unknown city. I knew in my heart that I could not leave my family at present. Time does not stand still for anyone. Elder members were becoming older and I didn't know the length of precious time that I would have left with them. I had also decided that I wanted my life with James here in the North East, in our home that we had managed to build and carve out together as a twosome and not in some rented, lifeless, faceless apartment. We have a life and are part of the community up here and I don't want to lose that sense of belonging.

As I sipped my tea further, I thought also that after we had attended the event and extravagance of Tim and Nora's wedding, which had so obviously divided her family members, I concluded that I wanted a solid start to marriage rather than just an impressive wedding. To me, the most important aspect of any wedding is the marriage and the vows that two people declare to each other in front of their most loved ones and the respect that those two people have for one another, something that I deeply wanted. James and I had still not made a final decision on our wedding and time was ticking on but that all changed following an unexpected visit from none other than Nora herself.

I was clearing up the well-used kitchen doing mundane ordinary day to day tasks, when the doorbell rang with its electronic tones. James was out watching football with his dad and I wasn't expecting anyone. I shrugged my shoulders nonchalantly as I wondered who it could be. As I opened the pastel-coloured front door to a gentle sea breeze, I was greeted by a beautiful bunch of pale pink roses, a packet of chocolate oat biscuits and a happy smiling face. Nora was stood in front of me and she asked if she could come in.

I nodded, albeit somewhat surprised by her unannounced visit, and led her into the little sun room at the rear of the house, put the kettle on and sat with my somewhat distanced old friend.

I must admit, Nora looked really great, a lot more like herself now. Gone was the gauntness which marred her face and she also looked much happier. The fact that she brought biscuits was a good sign in itself, I thought.

"How are you, Anna?" Nora asked a little awkwardly.

"I am fine, thanks. "It is good to see you," I replied warmly, as I carried in a tea tray with two patterned mugs of hot milky tea and a plate with the kindly gifted biscuits on.

Nora then continued, "I wanted to see you face-to-face, Anna, as I feel like I should say sorry and explain a bit about my behaviour recently. I realise now that the wedding made me go a bit crazy and I said and acted in ways which I shouldn't have."

I smiled at her unsurely as I tried to gauge if she wanted a reaction from me at this point but then Nora took a deep breath and carried on.

"I want to explain, Anna, I have always looked up to you. You have always been the most attractive, the cleverest and you have such a wonderful life with James who just simply adores you." I opened my mouth and tried to interject her opinions but Nora stopped me. "I guess you could say I have always been jealous of what you have and what you have achieved. I have always felt second best and then when I got engaged, which was the one thing which I felt was mine and which I did first, you and James then got engaged too."

I tried again to intervene but Nora was having none of it. She continued and looked downwards and somewhat shameful.

"I know it is ridiculous of me Anna, but I just wanted to be the first to be married and to have the big wedding and all the focus on me. I did exclude you and in doing so I have really hurt you, haven't I?"

I slowly nodded again but I was glad that Nora had realised she had been a bit elaborate with some of her behaviour recently.

"It's okay," I replied quietly. 'Weddings are meant to be stressful events. I am just pleased that you had a lovely day and had the wedding of your dreams."

Nora then looked down shyly at her feet and her perfectly manicured toes as she shuffled her sandals together on the sun room rug and confided, "Actually, there was a lot of things I didn't want and I would have preferred a much smaller wedding in all honesty. I felt like I just lost control, Anna; control of the happiest day of my life. Tim's family became so involved with every minute detail and I felt like I couldn't really say anything as they were paying for it all. They kept pushing me with their ideas, the time that was spent by them all and myself in planning the wedding to each tiny detail was insane and I felt like I had to go along with everything they suggested to keep them happy."

I felt so bad for Nora at this point and hadn't realised she had been feeling like this. I hugged my old friend and I was relieved that she no longer felt like skin and bone.

"You look a lot happier now, Nora, and you look healthier too, if you don't mind me saying. A lot more like your old self," I said delicately.

Nora smiled back at me and quietly replied, "That was the other thing, Anna. I realise now I took my dieting too far. Food was the only thing I felt like I could control and I found myself playing a strange game with myself to see how thin I could get. The thinner I got, the more rewarded I was in my control and then I wanted to push myself to my next weight target and it was becoming a dangerously unhealthy cycle."

I was pleased she had confided this.

"Oh Nora," I said with a caring sigh. "I wish you had come and spoken to me sooner and I could have tried to help you in some way."

Nora's sad eyes glistened and she looked uncomfortable but she also looked somewhat relieved that she had spoken to me in this way and that I had listened to her. There was an insecure silence in the room as she looked at me and I felt I needed to change the flow of the conversation.

"Anyhow," I said, "I am really interested in hearing all of your ideas. I bet you had some fantastic ones; why don't we change the subject and, as my bridesmaid, you can tell me what you think would be nice."

Nora chuckled and looked reassured and the two of us spent the afternoon laughing and giggling like old times in the quaint little sunlit back room, as we exchanged our various ideas until we were disturbed by a frazzled looking James arriving home for dinner and we realised what time it was.

I lay awake that night staring at the blank ceiling, as I thought more about my afternoon with Nora. It had been really lovely to see her and I was very pleased that she had apologised for her uncharacteristic behaviour recently. I genuinely hoped our friendship would recover to how it had once been, but I felt like it would be hard to get back to that point.

I had learnt a stark lesson from recent events and even though Nora would still be my bridesmaid and a dear friend to me and she was free to make her own choices, it had hurt me deeply that, in her eyes, I was merely a guest to her at her wedding and that I had played no part at all, not even in a small way, in any of her special day.

I thought increasingly more about my gran's cherished friendship and deep unbreakable bond with Nell; a friendship which had crossed over to become family and it upset me to think that I would probably never experience that, certainly not with my oldest childhood friend.

As I tossed and turned from side to side, my gran's gentle voice echoed in my mind as I thought about her own love story and the impact it had not only on her life, but on those around her. I finally fell asleep that night knowing that time was a treasured gift and a priceless commodity. I didn't want to spend countless hours planning the minutiae of a wedding, instead I wanted to celebrate the joy of mine and James love with my loved ones and an idea started to form from my nightly musings, I just hoped James would like it and be happy to go along with it.

The sun awoke and the new day began with freshly brewed coffee and buttery hot toast with James in the garden, sitting on our timeworn wicker garden furniture amongst the colourful flower pots which were dotted around our little patio sun trap. James sat and listened intently to my intended ideas about our wedding and when I had finished, his smile turned into a wide grin.

"I love it, Anna," James said happily. "And I love you. Do you really think we would have enough time to sort it all out though?"

I looked back at my husband to be and couldn't wait to do our wedding in our way.

"I really hope so," I replied excitedly.

James and I spent the next three hours frantically making numerous phone calls and emails to various suppliers. When we convened back in the garden just before midday, we exchanged ideas and we realised it was happening. We could do it; we were getting married in a mere seven weeks on the final weekend in August. I was so utterly excited, I leapt up into James's arms.

"Well, we had better tell our guests then," I said to James with elated joy.

That afternoon James and I went hastily from shop to printer to shop and back again and we carefully crafted out our first batch of our very own wedding invitations.

I knew, without any hesitation at all, where the first invitation would be hand-delivered.

As James and I pulled up to the honeysuckle-covered little cottage I really couldn't wait to go inside. My gran merrily opened the door to us and led us into the kitchen to put the kettle on whilst simultaneously producing a flowery plate with an array of biscuits on it. Then she summoned us all into the beautiful sea view garden along with her now finished and completed tea tray.

As we all sat together and the gentle breeze wafted through our hair, I eagerly handed my gran the crisp notelet which she daintily placed between her creased fingers. I observed intently as she lifted it slowly to her nose as if to try and inhale its contents, a habit of hers and then she carefully opened the creamy envelope. I watched as my gran's eyes darted about from word to word as she devoured the contents of the invitation, before she then focused on James and I and softly said, "My precious,

precious sweethearts," whilst holding the invitation tightly to her heart.

LILY

28th November 1946

As the light slowly began to filter into my childhood room and started awaking me from a tormented sleep, the realisation as to why I was there in the first place hit me. I couldn't even fathom the events which took place the day previously and I struggled to make any sense of them. I somehow mustered all my strength together to lift my heavy body out of bed, throw on some old clothes and forlornly made my way downstairs to the catastrophe that lay below me.

My dad, Harry and some of the villagers had already left much earlier to go to Fisherman's Cove to recommence the fraught search for Red which I desperately wanted to be a part of. I grabbed my old winter coat as my baby kicked me alarmingly and I hastily made my way out of the terrace, my mam shouting worriedly behind me and trying to stop me to come with me but I wanted and very much needed to go on my own.

I surveyed the merciless but now teasingly calm and gentle sea and felt anxious just looking at its cool stillness. The more I stared at the sea the more I found myself glaring angrily into the far-off darkened blue distance and the emptiness of the vast waters.

I was then somewhat taken aback by the sheer brightness of the sun that morning and the strange and rather bizarre way that the light reflected off Marsden Rock and into its quiet bay. I don't know what possessed me but in a trance-like daze I changed my direction and I didn't go to Fisherman's Cove.

Instead I went to those welcoming white washed steps which eerily beckoned me towards them and down to our beach, Marsden beach. The beach directly under our village.

I carefully climbed down each small step, descending deeper through the weathered cliff whilst holding on to the makeshift rope rail, until I finally reached the bottom. I could see a light illuminating The Beach Grotto and I could see the landlord sweeping up broken glass, damage no doubt caused by the storm. I cautiously stepped onto the sand and I started to fear the very worst outcome of this search.

In the pit of my stomach, I thought Red would not have made the distance to our beach in the storm but I still aimlessly wandered the full length of the bay and back again, retracing my steps and looking behind every jutting out rock face and into every sad pool of displaced sea water.

I knelt on the sand of this lonesome beach and I silently wept. I mourned my courtship with Red, I mourned my marriage to Red and finally, I mourned our future together and the life that Red and I had planned out. I sat in complete isolation on the sunken wet sand with my head in my hands, until the baby kicked me as if out of concern and to comfort me and I realised I would have to make a new future now. I screamed out desperately in pain at the sea as I felt like my heart was spiralling away in tiny pieces into its desolate vastness. How could I possibly live without Red and bring up his child without him being there by my side to be a part of it?

I felt nauseous, uneasy and exhausted following my outburst and I wanted to sit down properly. I slowly made my way back up the sandy beach and teetered precariously onto the row of rounded weathered pebbles which separated the sand from the cliffs, until I reached the cave, a place of comfort. I thought I would sit there in the cave quietly for a moment in my area of solace, my childhood friend and my adult matchmaker, gather my thoughts and get my breath back.

I gradually crept up to the blackened hole, entered the faithful entrance and walked with a stooped bow to the ledge to climb up into the hidden crevice. I found myself standing in the darkness and a realisation overcame me, this place in which I sought such comfort and solace had suddenly lost its former magic. Gone was the sound of childhood laughter and harmony, gone was the thrill of new young love and gone was the hope of a future, instead what lay before me was a black empty, wet, lonely, and unfriendly space.

I decided to persist to rest and I pulled myself up onto the ledge to the point where the air in the cave transformed from salty dampness to musky dryness and into a somewhat surprising and very dim light. I peered upwards and wondered how there could be a light in here. My eyes steadily grew accustomed to the dullness until I was able to focus on the contents of the cave and I could see an odd formation. In this space which I knew very well, there was something which was out of place.

There was a strange piled mound in the corner; it looked like a collection of rags or clothes. I wondered if something or even someone was living in the cave. I cautiously approached the mound, not sure whether to continue or not, my pulse racing at the unknown and potential of danger but as I crept closer, I gasped as I realised this mound of rags was moving ever so slightly. I carefully and quietly neared the mound and realised as I grew closer that they hid the unmistakable outline of a person. My heart pounded faster as simultaneously small beads of sweat formed and then dripped down my forehead as I gradually lowered back the sandy-coloured cloth that would reveal the face and identity of the stranger.

I was speechless as I caught my breath and could not believe what I saw as it was a face that I recognised, a face which I knew intimately and a face which I loved dearly. It was a true miracle, the face of my loving husband stared back and I lowered myself to my Red. I placed my hands on his face as he reacted to my touch. He was breathing gently but looked very weak. I noticed that he was wrapped up in one of our blankets.

His beautiful eyes looked up at me sadly with a slightly glazed look of desperation.

"Lil," he whispered painfully between breaths. I sobbed over him. "I just wanted to see you one last time, please forgive me. I love you."

I didn't understand his words and what he was trying to convey to me. He sounded like he was saying goodbye. I urgently needed to go and get help but he begged me to stay with him. He only wanted to see me and I couldn't bear to leave him on his own in this way. I held his frightened hand tightly as he lay there quietly in that dim light just looking up at me whilst trying to conceal his pain from me. The blanket which protected him fell awkwardly from over his body and I could see that he was naked under it and his chest was badly bruised. I pulled the blanket back up to cover him and stroked his russet hair.

"You will be okay," I whispered to him. "I am here now."

He looked deeply into my eyes as he tried to explain. "I am so sorry, Lil. The lifeboats were damaged and me and the other navy boys knew we couldn't all fit into them. There were too many people in them for their size. Did the boats even manage to make it to shore?" I nodded silently.

Red let out a sigh of relief and managed a little smile and continued, "I knew I had to swim and the only thing I could think of was you and I knew you would be in the lighthouse. I swam against the current, towards the light and onto the beach. I knew you would come to the cave, to our cave."

Red squeezed my hand and then clutched his chest in pain. His skin felt cold, so I took my warm coat off and placed it around him. Red held my hand back, as I brought myself nearer to him, as I placed my body next to his. Red's expression changed to astonishment as he looked at my rounded tummy. I had forgotten that he didn't know he was going to be a father. I smiled at him, pulled him close and placed his cold hand on my tummy.

"Lil," Red exclaimed in bewilderment.

I put my finger gently on his lips and softly said, "I wanted it to be a surprise. You are going to be a daddy."

I placed both his hands fully around my bump now and lay my body next to his and clasped him into my arms as our baby kicked his hands. I murmured into Red's ear,

"See you have everything to live for my darling. We love you."

We lay like that together – the three of us in the dullness – for what seemed like hours. Red's body gradually started to warm up but he kept wincing and clutching at his chest in pain. I stroked his hair and kissed his face, humming to him softly like my mam did to me when I was little. I talked to him about everything I could think of: the baby, Honeysuckle, our families, Nell and Harry and about our future together, until one moment, he didn't nod back.

Hot silent tears burned my face one by one, as I lay flopped against him, my life, my one and only love. The cave was dispersed into an unnerving stillness and no longer held the tranquil properties that I once sought from it. I felt very small, alone and lost. I tried to think back to the day I met Red and how the path that my life had been following had been altered indescribably by that one chance meeting. I could hear something sounding in the distance which overwhelmed the silence but I was not leaving Red, a shrill call, perhaps from a seabird which was cruelly shattering my domain.

As pacing footsteps came up behind me and preceded to physically lift me off the ground, I realised it was Nell and Harry. They were too late. I was in another place now, a serene place of calmness and still. I could see their lips moving on their distressed faces but words just didn't make sense and I saw Nell run out the cave. I don't really know what happened next, one minute I was lying with my Red in the cave and the next Nell and Harry had shouted at me loudly to go to The Beach Grotto which still had glass on its floor. So, I did. I don't know why I had to sit there with Mr Colman the landlord, but I did. I sipped at the sugary drink that had been made for me as I counted all the bits of shattered glass on the floor; a reflection, I thought, of my life at that very moment.

I could hear the lift shaft whirring mechanically in the distance and I moved towards it, stepping over all of the broken pieces of glass which on close inspection looked eerily beautiful in their many translucent colours. I found myself suddenly blinded by a vivid bright white light as the lift doors opened. An unworldly creature, an angel, stepped out. The serene lady was calling my name repeatedly to find me and come and collect me. I was very relieved by the instruction and found that I was glad to go with her and to leave the broken glass and mess behind me.

It was then that I realised, as I calmly embraced the body of the spirit, that this was my mam and she had come to take me home.

ANNA

26ᵗʰ August 2017

The day had finally arrived, and the sun shone brightly to mark the start of the hazy late summer bank holiday weekend. I could scarcely believe today was the culmination of mine and James's love and the day that our families would join together. I had only two instructions for my parents for the day, one was to simply enjoy it and the other was to provide bacon sandwiches. I knew the second request had already been fulfilled by the mouth-watering scent which filled the house as I went downstairs. Nora had also just arrived to help me get ready and to get herself sorted and as we sat around the table devouring our breakfast washed down with pink champagne – we are classy Northern lasses after all. With laughter filling the room, myself, my parents, and my old friend, I knew today would be a good day.

I hadn't been one to dream about a wedding dress when I was a little girl but I had found it very easy to pick my dress. I had decided to do this on my own due to the short timeframe, so I was intrigued to see what everyone's reaction would be. Nora had changed into the lemon-coloured chiffon dress that I had chosen for her with a dressing gown thrown over the top for now, whilst a professional hair and make-up artist attended to our needs, my sheer decadence of the day.

As we sat there together getting beautified, Nora turned to me and said, "I so wish I had listened to my instincts for my wedding, Anna. This morning has just been lovely with your family and so personal in your old home. I don't want to sound ungrateful to Tim as I love the bones off him and his family too, but I wish we had got married up here. Your day is going to be so meaningful to you all."

Nora then proceeded to pass the two newly filled champagne glasses that we had brought up from breakfast as she turned to me and said, "To you and James."

The morning progressed in haste. My golden tresses had been strategically curled off to one side and pinned around at the back whilst I wore a deep red on my lips and I knew it had reached the time to put my wedding dress on. I carefully stepped into my 1920s style strappy silk and lace dress which hugged my curves at the top and then fell loosely down to the floor. I loved it just as much now as the first time I ever saw it. I had asked everyone to wait downstairs for me and I proceeded to put on my jewelled flat sandals so that I could make my descent to my family.

As I entered the living room my mam gasped, my dad looked proud and Nora clapped, then a familiar gentle voice from the corner of the room calmly said, "Our Anna, our beautiful star."

My little gran was sitting there looking resplendent in her crimson outfit with sheer glee in her eyes. "Come over here, pet," she said.

I went to her and she took my hand in hers as she handed me a brown paper bag. "Open it," she said with her kind voice.

As I carefully peeled down the wrinkled paper of the bag, I could see a flash of light as mother of pearl peeped out and as I delved further, the paper unwrapped to show my gran's great grandmother's hair slide. I was taken aback. I knew my mam had worn this when she married my dad but when I asked about it both her and my gran had coyly pretended it had become broken over its lifespan. I was so pleased and grateful that this heirloom remained in the family.

"It is yours now," my gran said as she carefully placed the intricate slide into my curls.

My mam, gran and Nora, resplendent in their finery, then went to get into the first car to take them to St Andrew's Church in Marsden and my dad and I got into the wedding car. I was starting to feel nervous now, as the car went along the glistening sea front, past the grassy headland and past the majestic Souter until we reached the lovely little church which was basking in the sunlight. I stepped out of the car with my loyal dad and walked arm in arm to the door of the church. I could see my wedding flowers at the entrance of the church and I felt calmer. As I entered the church with my dad, I was so proud of my family as I looked upon the row upon row of smiling faces which were interspersed with the resplendent and meaningful sight of red lilies everywhere. I looked up the aisle towards where my beloved would be standing as another flash of red caught my eye first.

My eyes slowly began to focus to become accustomed to the filtered sunlight which beamed through the colourful stained-glass windows. I could make out the shadowy figures which stood either side of the aisle. Firstly, my parents, then James's parents and then there at the front with pride of place standing smartly in his best suit next to my gran in her crimson outfit, was my granddad, rays of light reflecting off the last remaining russet tones in his hair.

The wedding in St Andrew's Church in Marsden – the very same church which held the history of my family, where my parents married and my grandparents before them – now marked the beginning of mine and James's marriage and I could not think of a more significant or special place for me and James to say our vows to one another. As we made our lifetime commitment to each other, I felt proud, proud to be James's wife, proud to stand in front of my Lily and my Red and proud to be standing on this hallowed ground.

My husband and I left the church with our family and friends as we piled into cheery sunset yellow bunting decorated double-decker buses and made our way along the coast towards the point where the headland jutted out. I took a moment as we past Souter again, I winked at my old friend, as the late afternoon sun shone brightly and illuminated its red and white glory. As we went by the open grassy field at the base of the lighthouse I looked out to the endless sea and thought how different this space could have been, I knew my gran and granddad's hearts would always belong to Marsden and I looked over at them as they sat together hand in hand and still very much in love after all this time.

The horn on the bus made a sharp honk as we reached the destination. As James and I departed the bus we looked out at the hundreds upon hundreds of seabirds who circled and dove in the hot summer air in and out of the glazed North Sea and the imposing shadow of Marsden Rock. I took James's hand to go to our wedding reception and I lead him towards the covered awning and into the tunnel which said three simple words: 'The Beach Grotto'.

We made our way downward to the bay where The Beach Grotto was decorated in rich and bright Caribbean colours with red lilies dotted around everywhere and marking a path to the double doors which led straight out on to the veranda and onto Marsden beach. James and I had succeeded in bringing the Caribbean to the North East and we were so very, very lucky with the weather. We had arranged for the beach to be cordoned off for our wedding guests and for our dance floor to be directly on the beach. Our guests looked happy as the tropical sounds of steel drums echoed across the bay and into the waters. Waiting staff mingled between guests with various seasoned chicken, fish and vegetarian delicacies, paired alongside rum cocktails, before The Beach Grotto fired up the grills for a very informal beach BBQ with fresh seafood, caught and marinated in coconut and spices that very day. As day became night I was so pleased with mine and James's decision to have our day our way but with a nod to the past. As I looked at my beloved husband's handsome face I realised how utterly special he was in allowing the day to happen just like we wanted. My thoughts were interrupted by the sound of our wedding band, who along with the musicians on the steel drums, were calling James and I to the dance floor. My husband took my hand and the lush reggae tones vibrated in the sand as we moved our bodies side by side in perfect harmony with one another. James held me closer and whispered softly in my ear, "Anna, I love your way. I love you."

I laughed, and he then spun me in the sand with my flowing dress moving in momentum, we then invited everyone else onto the dance floor to share our moment.

I looked over at my grandparents who were off to the side of the dance floor and gently swaying side to side with each other as the vibrant music played. They looked in their own private realm with not a care in the world as my granddad took my gran's hand and spun her in her crimson dress, almost looking like two shadows moving against the backdrop of Marsden Rock. I was so pleased I was able to give them this moment, as I knew this would be special for them. As James held me to him closely, I savoured this very moment. I took a deep breath and I looked up to the stars and then my eyes were drawn to the top of the cliff where the open grassy space lay. I realised it was exactly seventy-one years, three months and one day between my grandparents' wedding and our wedding. I wondered if the ancestors of the village were watching and if they could see Lily and Red dance on Marsden beach again. I hoped that they were happy that I arranged this day as a dedication to my grandparents, to love and also to them. I wished they were happy anyhow and I imagined them up there in their old village, the last village, in their finery and having a right old knees up. I giggled as James smiled at me. "What's so funny?" he said.

"Nothing that concerns you," I laughed as I grabbed his hand again. "Come on husband, let's dance!"

The evening remained light for some time and as the party continued I could see my invincible grandparents starting to tire and wanting to say their goodbyes to depart back to Honeysuckle. James hugged them both and then I led them back into the faithful Beach Grotto and to the little lift shaft. I placed both of their hands between mine and softly said to them both, "Thank you."

My gran replied in her soft voice, "For what, pet?"

I held their hands together tightly and said, "For this. For loving each other and sharing your story with me and for teaching me about love and what love can mean, and for inspiring this very day."

I hugged them both as I placed my gran's hand back into my granddad's and they went into the lift together hand in hand. The lift doors closed leaving me alone and I thought more about my words and how important love was, especially in this generation when sometimes love could be belittled or even laughed at and forgotten. I suddenly felt sad for those people who would not find or come close to what my grandparents have and how I hoped James and I would live to have an everlasting love like theirs. I made my way happily back to the veranda and knew that James, my family and my roots meant everything to me and I was so honoured to have experienced such a meaningful day. I reached out my arm to the glossy wooden double door to the veranda and pulled it open as I stepped out into the light.

EPILOGUE

29th August 2017

A few days had passed since the wedding. James and I were blissful happy newlyweds and the seafront still basked in glorious sunshine. I had arranged to take my gran out for some ice cream whilst my granddad, who was not such a big ice cream lover now, stayed behind to do some gardening. I pulled up in my little car and parked next to the charming yellow cottage and walked past the established roses as my granddad spotted me and opened the cottage door.

"Come in, our love," he said cheerfully in his deep voice. "Your gran is just gathering her things together, she won't be a moment."

I looked around the sunlit hall and took in my surroundings which summarised my grandparents' life together; the lovely curiosities which were lined up on the little wooden shelves, a fresh bouquet of lilies standing tall in a red glass vase on a doily, the shiny brass ships bell which was nailed to the stair banister, a black cast iron silhouette of a miner, as well as the endless family photos which covered the walls. I loved looking at the photos of my mam when she was little. Rose in the roses, was one of my gran's favourites, whilst my Auntie Amelia, who was just a baby at the time, calmly sat next to her. There was one photo which moved me every time due to the sheer happiness on my grandparents' faces; the two of them sat together, skins bronzed with their arms draped casually around each other and with flower garlands around their necks as they clinked their embossed fluted wine glasses together which in tiny letters read 'Curacao'.

"Anna," my gran chirped "I'm ready."

My gran gave me a smile and laughed as she caught me looking at the anniversary photo again. She laughed again as she sighed happily and declared, "Our paradise. He always promised me he would take me there. Only took him fifty years, but it was worth the wait."

I linked my gran's arm as I helped her to the car and got her comfortable in the front passenger seat. We drove out of her street and along the coast road. It must always be strange I thought for my gran to pass along this path and I could see this etched in her face. These roads carried a lot of happiness for her but also a lot of sadness about what used to be. Her head bowed slightly as we went past the remaining sturdy wrought iron gates of the old village school which had long been demolished; the school which she had worked so hard for and built up, which culminated in her becoming headmistress. As we past the lighthouse and the open grassy space which once housed a thriving community I could see a sort of longing in her eyes which would glaze before being replaced with a coy little smile as she fell contentedly into her memories.

I pulled up to the ice cream hut which was always open, come rain or come shine, and bought two 99's before I drove the car along the road which was on the outskirts of the old village and parked in the quiet car park which at one point would have had a terraced street on it.

My gran and I enjoyed our ice creams in harmonious silence as we looked out towards the glistening deep blue waters of the North Sea watching the waves bob up and down and the seabirds circling the rock. I wanted to know more about her story as I had learnt so much from her but I wanted to know more and the ending, I took her hand and gently said, "Gran, please tell me, what happened after you found granddad?" Her wise faced turned to me and she began in her soft voice.

"The last thing I remember about that day was Red's eyes closing and being unable to wake him. I then must have fallen into a confusion as Nell and Harry appeared out of nowhere and started shouting at me to go to The Beach Grotto. What I remembered after that was Nell ran back with me to The Beach Grotto and it was in here that she collected all the spare blankets and coats from the pub and got Mr Colman, the landlord, to go back to the cave with her but not before he had managed to summon someone to get an ambulance to the top of the cliff. The three of them, Nell, Harry and Mr Colman, managed to carry Red's limp body all the way out the cave across the shingle part of the beach and into The Beach Grotto before getting him into the lift and up to the cliff top where many others from the village had turned up to help. I was with my mam at home at this point and I genuinely believed that I had lost him."

My gran sighed and took a deep breath and continued. "As the evening dusk fell that night I was still no wiser to Red's condition and things remained this way until a tired-looking Harry came to my parents' door. Him and Nell had been at the old South Shields General Hospital with Red for the entire day and that the doctors there had concluded that Red had several broken ribs and had caught a chill to his chest and passed out with the pain. The doctors did state that if it wasn't for Red's quick thinking in removing all the wet clothes, covering himself in the dry blanket in our warm cave and drinking the sugary lemonade, he would without a doubt have died of hypothermia that very night. At this point I didn't know what to say, I wanted to shout with glee that my love was alright but I also wanted to burst into tears and march straight to the hospital to be with Red. The time came the next morning for that however, as Red stayed in hospital for a further three weeks until he was deemed fit enough to come home to me, the village and to Honeysuckle.

"You see, my dear, it really was a mixture of the glow of a lighthouse, the assistance of a tight-knit community and the pastimes of two little girls and a boy from the village on the cliff who by leaving their treasures in their childhood cave saved my love's life."

"Oh gran," I said as I held her close and could smell the fragrant lily of the valley perfume in her hair. I smiled at her. "Gran, can I ask, whatever happened to Nell and Harry? They were such close friends of yours and granddad but I don't think I ever met them or have even seen a photo of them?"

My gran reached slowly into her bag and pulled out her navy-blue worn purse and carefully extracted a black and white photo out of the stitched lining of it. It was a photo of her wedding day of her and my granddad standing in front of Marsden Rock, its arch still intact, and they were smiling with two others.

"This is Harry and this is Nell, Anna," she said as she pointed sorrowfully to the faces in the photo.

"I keep them in here close to me at all times. Come and walk with me for a moment," said my gran quietly.

I helped my gran out of the car and she linked my arm and led me slowly over the open grass, the breeze gently blowing her hair and along the cliff heading towards the lighthouse. As we approached the base of where the lighthouse has its garden, I could see a patch of long marram grass which my gran was directing me towards.

"This used to be where the allotments were, but it has the best view of the sea from here," my gran said softly.

As we got nearer to the grass I could see a wooden bench which had been partially hidden behind the longer grasses. My gran took my hand at this point. "Come and sit with me, Anna," she said.

We waded through the spiky grass until we reached our destination – the old wooden bench. My gran took a deep breath and palely looked out to sea before pulling an embroidered lily handkerchief out of her sleeve and, wiping her eye, she then took the handkerchief and very carefully rubbed at the centre of the bench to reveal two golden plaques. Once she was finished she turned to me with a sadness in her eyes and simply said, "Read."

I looked at the collection of heartfelt letters and felt a lump in my throat form as I slowly read each one aloud from the first plaque:

Nell Gunn 1927-1982
'To my darling wife Nell,
the love of my life,
my light has gone out,
all my love forever, Harry.'

My gran then squeezed my hand as my voice trembled as I then read out the second plaque:

Harry Gunn 1927-1983
'To our dear and much loved friend Harry,
reunited now with your Nell,
our memories will never fade,
all our love, Lily and Red'

I cried as I hugged my gran as she wiped a tear away from her own face and we held each other like that for a few minutes.

My gran, ever the strong lady, then composed herself to explain. "Nell got ill, Anna, so very ill and the illness just ravaged her body. It was just an awful, awful time. I will never ever forget the day she died, she was but a shell of her former self and the fight in her just went out. Harry was beside himself and utterly consumed with grief, I think his heart was too broken and he just didn't want to be here without Nell. He just gave up on life and passed away three months after her. They are always in my heart,

Anna and not a day goes by when I don't think of them both. I used to come here a lot with your granddad and we would just sit and think about our friends and watch the seabirds on the rock playfully darting in and out of the arch before it was demolished. The seabirds always make me think of them. The admiration of Nell's sheer determination to save those baby birds, paired with the horror on Harry's face when she did her 'rescues' is one of my fond memories, I like to think that Nell is up there watching over her birds, her legacy, whilst Harry sits by watching over her in the shadow of the lighthouse."

As I looked at the birds and then up to the sky, I helped my gran get up from the bench and I said softly, "I think they will be doing exactly that gran."

As my gran and I made our way back to my car along the gravelly path I had one final question for my gran. "After everything, gran, how could you bear for granddad to go back to sea for all those years? I don't think I would have been strong enough to let James out of my sight if that had been him."

My gran turned to me and faced me straight on and said to me the wisest words I have ever heard. "You must never ever be afraid and do not live your life in fear, Anna. You must always face your fears boldly and straight on and push for what you want."

I nodded and looked at this incredible woman and the experiences she had had in her life. A woman I was proud and honoured to call my gran.

As I took one last look at the field we would cross to get back to the car I wondered if people really knew the hidden depths of this land and the love and friendships which were built here. My gran had now shared her memories with me and I knew what had happened here but I would not live forever and with me, perhaps her memories would die.

I vowed to myself that I would not allow this and I would keep the memory of Marsden Village alive. For me and the family that lay ahead in my future, this sparse but beautiful piece of land would never be just the bit of unnamed empty grass next to the lighthouse, instead it would always and forever be the village of our ancestors, Marsden.

* * *

Marsden Village was built by the Whitburn Coal Company in the 1870s and was a thriving community. However, by the 1960s the village had been demolished following a Category D rating from the Development Plan Board, making it the last of its kind in South Tyneside to be fully demolished. In 2018 there is no trace that a village existed in this grassy space except for the odd piece of brick which is hidden in long grasses. The space is now owned and protected by The National Trust.

* * *

Marsden Rock was a naturally formed arch which succumbed to tidal erosion in 1996 causing the arch to collapse and splitting the rock into two stacks. By 1997, the second stack was declared unsafe for the public and was demolished. The rock and its surrounding area now holds the status of being the largest mainland breeding colony of seabirds between the Tweed and the Tees rivers, second only to the Farne Islands in Northumberland.

AUTHORS NOTE

Although the characters in *The Last Village* are a work of fiction the setting in which they move in is not.
The socio-historical location of the novel has always greatly intrigued me; including the significant impact it made to the people and the landscape of the North East of England. The beautiful local coastal geography has also inspired the setting for the novel.

It is also worth mentioning that I have made use of artistic licence and both places and names, past and current, have been changed to enhance the story.

I also claim all bent truths and errors of fact as my own.

ABOUT THE AUTHOR

Audla English grew up in the North East of England. Born in Sunderland, a graduate of Newcastle University and living in South Tyneside, she is passionate about this wonderful region.

You can find more information about Audla and her books at:

www.audlaenglish.co.uk

Or connect with her online at:
- Twitter: https://twitter.com/AudlaE
- Facebook: http://www.facebook.com/audla.english.5

If you enjoyed *The Last Village*, please consider leaving a review:
- www.amazon.co.uk
- www.amazon.com
- www.goodreads.com

30975061R00127

Printed in Poland
by Amazon Fulfillment
Poland Sp. z o.o., Wrocław